Thaddeus Bix

and the Pirates of Pepperjack

Kylie Mansfield

First published in Australia in 2016
by Meraki Books – www.merakibooks.com
Copyright © Kylie Mansfield

ISBN 978-0-9945209-0-6 (print book) |
978-0-9945209-2-0 (epub) | 978-0-9945209-1-3 (Kindle)

Cover Illustration – Nathan Jurevicius
Cover Design – Luke Jurevicius
Author Photo – Shot from the Heart photography
http://shotfromtheheart.com

National Library of Australia Cataloguing-in-Publication entry:
Creator: Mansfield, Kylie, author.
Title: Thaddeus Bix and the Pirates of Pepperjack / Kylie Mansfield ; edited by Nicola O'Shea ; cover illustrations by Nathan Jurevicius ; cover layout by Luke Jurevicius.

ISBN: 9780994520906 (paperback)

Series: Mansfield, Kylie. Thaddeus Bix ; book 1.
Other Creators/Contributors: O'Shea, Nicola, editor.
Jurevicius, Nathan, 1973- illustrator.
Jurevicius, Luke, book designer.

Dewey Number: A823.4

For my brother Matthew James,
who loved stories and always told the
funniest ones of all.

I shall miss you on all of life's new
adventures ... xx

CONTENTS

CHAPTER ONE

PIRATES AND SHADOWS

Thaddeus Bix was taking the long way home again, his heart heavy in his chest and his mind a whirr of unhappy thoughts. He pedalled his bike speedily along the Esplanade, feeling the ocean wind blowing his scruffy red hair off his freckled face and tangling it into a striking resemblance of a bird's nest. He had almost reached the end of the Esplanade's wooden planks when he heard something peculiar. Something that sounded a lot like cannon fire.

He slammed on his brakes and came to a skidding halt at the end of the rock wall that divided the sandy beach from the boardwalk. When he looked out to sea, he almost fell off his bike. There, like a fat splotch of ink on a postcard picture, was a big black wooden pirate ship with a black flag that bore a menacing skull and crossbones.

Thaddeus stared, rubbed his eyes, and stared some more. The splotch on the ocean remained. He was pondering this fact when he realised something even more peculiar. He was the only person who'd seemed to notice the pirate ship. No one else was paying it any attention at all.

He looked back towards the ship, thinking that maybe his dark thoughts had conjured it – but no, it was still there. What was more, a longboat holding eight pirates was being lowered over its side. As he watched, the longboat splashed into the water and its occupants began steadily rowing to shore.

Thaddeus froze. A tingling of unease flowed through him. It was the same feeling he got whenever his parents tried to encourage him down onto the sand and near the water.

An elderly man walking his dog must have sensed Thaddeus's worry for he stopped and said kindly, 'You alright, sonny?'

'Can you see it?' asked Thaddeus, pointing towards the ship.

The elderly man followed his finger, then swivelled his head to look left and right along the line of the horizon. 'See what?'

'The pirate ship – and those pirates there!'

Thaddeus's finger was now pointing to the beach, where the longboat had landed and four filthy pirates were splashing their way ashore.

'I think you've spent too much time in the heat, sonny. Best you be away home now before you start imagining anything else,' the man said with a chuckle. He guided his dog away from where it was energetically sniffing Thaddeus's front tyre and the pair continued their walk along the Esplanade.

The pirates were halfway to the rock wall now and Thaddeus could see them distinctly. The pirate in the lead had an ugly face with a flat nose that looked as if it had been stuck on sideways. If this was all coming from Thaddeus's imagination, it was doing a pretty good job.

The pirates paused and scanned the beach. *Maybe they're looking for treasure*, thought Thaddeus, dropping his bike and leaning over the rock wall to look down at the sand. His movement must have caught the pirates' attention because they all stared directly at him. Suddenly he felt like a chook trapped in a henhouse with four foxes.

It was then Thaddeus decided it was time he went home. Quickly.

He jumped on his bike and was about to kick off when the pirate with the flat nose leapt over the wall and landed directly in the path of his front wheel. One beefy fist grabbed Thaddeus's handlebars. The other hand produced a nasty-looking old-fashioned pistol, which the pirate rested menacingly against his bulging belly.

'Got ye now, ye snivellin' brat,' he sneered, and gave a triumphant grin that showed off his miserable array of rotting teeth. The other three pirates crowded up beside him and he added, 'Look at 'im, Silver – he be the one! A perfect specimen. Where shall I shove 'im then?'

Silver was a squat little man with a barrel-like body and a face so engulfed by a bushy beard that only his piercing black eyes were visible. To Thaddeus, they looked like two small black beetles hiding within an equally black bush. Tucked into Silver's waist sash next to a shiny cutlass was an even bigger and nastier pistol. Its barrel was polished to perfection and gleamed threateningly in the afternoon sunlight. He was clearly the leader, for the other pirates were waiting on his orders.

'Ye can start by puttin' away yer pistol, Booth. We don't be wantin' any nosy people interferin' now, do we?' snapped Silver.

He walked awkwardly forwards and Thaddeus saw that he wore a wooden peg where his left leg should have been.

'You'd better hope nobody else saw you with that gun,' said Thaddeus, hoping the old man with the dog would turn around, see he was under attack and set his dog on the pirates.

'There bain't be many who be seein' us, laddie. Just children, 'cause they believe in anythin', and maybe a few adults who still believe in magic. They bain't be admittin' to it though, else people be thinkin' they be bonkers!'

The other pirates laughed loudly.

Shoving Booth away from the handlebars, Silver strutted in a wide circle around Thaddeus and his bike, finally coming to a stop in front of him and allowing his beetle-eyes to crawl intently over every inch of Thaddeus's body. He gave Thaddeus the heebie-jeebies.

Then Silver's whiskers twitched, hinting at a smile that caused Thaddeus to shiver. Not the kind of shiver you get on Christmas morning, but the kind that comes when you hear an unusual sound on a dark and stormy night.

'What did I be tellin' ye, ye scurvy dogs?' said Silver. 'The wizard knows what he be talkin' about. He be tellin' us we need to find a child to lead us to our Captain – and this laddie, he be the one, I be feelin' it in me bones. This laddie be our beacon to our Captain, me hearties.'

To Thaddeus, he said, 'Come 'ere, boy, we bain't about to hurt ye.'

Thaddeus wasn't born yesterday.

'You think it's gonna be that easy? If you want me, you'll have to come and get me – right after I tell the coppers.'

With that, he spun his bike around and took off at top speed back along the Esplanade.

The pirates were momentarily stunned into silence. By the time they had gathered their wits, Thaddeus had a record head-start.

'GET AFTER 'IM, YE FLEA-RIDDEN LUMPS, OR WE'LL ALL BE FEELIN' THE WRATH OF PEPPERJACK'S CURSE!' screamed Silver.

Thaddeus left the Esplanade and spun onto the street. Halfway along, the pirates began gaining on him. Thaddeus couldn't believe how fast they were. He cut through an alleyway and back towards school – there was no way he was going to lead them to his house.

He jumped his bike off the kerb, his tyres sliding along a storm drain grille before gripping the bitumen again. His chest was beginning to burn with effort, and when he reached the bottom of the hill he spun his head to see how close the ragged bunch were.

Silver was in the lead, which was surprising as he was the shortest and only had one leg. But then as Thaddeus watched, Silver leapt off the kerb and landed smack in the middle of the storm drain grille, where he came unstuck – literally. The narrow end of his wooden peg caught between the grille's metal rungs and the sudden stop sent him catapulting through the air like a giant tumbleweed on a windy day. He roared with surprise, did a few somersaults along the asphalt, and came to a skidding halt a short distance away, where he lay flapping like a hairy turtle upside down on its shell.

The other three pirates flying down the hill had no chance of stopping in time. They plummeted straight into their unfortunate leader, causing a pile-up worse than a peak-hour traffic jam. Silver immediately let rip with curses and punches, slamming a fist into Booth's eye. The pirates yelled and writhed as they tried to untangle themselves from one another.

Thaddeus stood a short way off, laughing at the spectacle. But when Silver bashed Booth over the head and sent him scurrying after the peg, which was wedged upright in the grille like a lone cricket stump, Thaddeus decided it was time to leave.

'Serves you right!' he yelled, kicking off and pedalling furiously homewards. He would get his mum to call the coppers – they'd deal with the pirates for sure.

With that thought in mind, he zigzagged happily along the road, the air whistling past his thin body and whipping his hair back like the tail of a flaming comet. He skirted a lamppost, hooned around a corner and over a ditch, and the scrabble of furious shouts behind him became fainter and fainter. A grin, thick as butter, spread across his face. What losers. As if they could ever catch him.

***

At the turn-off to his street, Thaddeus spun around to check that no filthy pirates were on his tail. Satisfied that he had lost them, he turned the corner. He was nearing his house when he saw his father's car reverse out of the driveway. That was something new. The car hadn't been parked there for weeks, not since Dad had moved out. Hope flared in Thaddeus's heart. Maybe everything was back to normal.

'Dad!' he yelled, and pedalled faster.

But his father didn't see him, and by the time Thaddeus reached the driveway he'd already driven off.

Thaddeus felt a heaviness fill his chest. He dropped his bike against the hedge and cut across the lawn, the pirates forgotten. Maybe he could ask Mum to call Dad so he could come back.

He flung open the front door and was about to yell out 'Hello' when he heard a sob coming from the living room. He froze, his heart skipping a beat.

Quietly he shut the front door, laid his school bag gently by the hall table and tiptoed towards the living room. He peeked around the doorframe and saw his mother perched on the edge of the sofa, her face buried in her hands. Thaddeus wasn't sure what to do. His mum had been sad and edgy for weeks, but he hadn't seen her cry before.

'Mum, what's wrong?' he asked as he stepped warily into the room. Fear snaked through his veins like poison, making his legs feel like heavy lumps of wood.

His mother looked up, startled, and tried unsuccessfully to wipe the tears off her cheeks.

Thaddeus crept towards her, trying to ignore the fearful coils tightening around his heart in a disgustingly uncomfortable manner. He could see that something was wrong … very, *very* wrong.

'What's happened?' he asked uncertainly. 'Is it Dad?'

His mother nodded, unable to squeeze out any words between her fresh sobs.

Tiny beads of sweat popped out all over Thaddeus's body and the air within the living room suddenly felt hot and heavy.

'What is it, Mum? Just tell me.'

She stared vacantly at his face.

Thaddeus saw all her familiar features but didn't recognise her. The panic that had been building within him suddenly pounded through his chest and roared into his ears, blocking out all sound. His eyes became filmy and his breath snagged in his throat.

'Just tell me, Mum,' he croaked, but as he put an arm around her stooped shoulders, he felt without being told that the worse that could happen had happened. Even though Thaddeus had wished and hoped every day that his father would come back, he knew now that he was never coming back – not to live with them anyway.

He felt the coils of fear tighten in his chest and worried his heart might crack under the pressure, like an egg held too tightly in someone's hand. He wanted to say something, but there was a lump in his throat that blocked any words. If only he'd pedalled faster and had managed to see his dad before he drove away. Maybe Dad would have changed his mind if Thaddeus had asked him to stay.

Silence hung heavily between Thaddeus and his mother like a fat thundercloud, thick and suffocating, punctuated only by the ticking of the grandfather clock. Until his mother began sobbing again.

'It'll be okay, Mum,' Thaddeus said, patting her shoulder gently. But the words felt like a lie. They stuck to his tongue and made it feel all pasty, like the craft glue they used at school.

Fresh tears spurted from her glazed and swollen eyes. 'I'm sorry, Thaddeus … but your father and I … it's not what we planned for our life … We had dreams once … plans for what our life would be like … Now those dreams are broken, like fallen stars …'

Pain tore through Thaddeus's chest and into his throat, and he looked away. He heard a distant cracking sound, like the shattering of a glass and then everything fell quiet, as if someone had thrown a big blanket over the world, draping it in complete silence. Even the grandfather clock had stopped ticking.

When Thaddeus turned back to his mum, he

saw that she was slumped against the back of the sofa, as if someone had cast a sleeping spell over her.

'Mum!' he said, panicked. He prodded her, but she didn't wake.

As he wondered what to do, and what had happened, he glimpsed a shadow moving on the wall. Hope burst through his mind like a ray of sunshine. He turned towards the doorway, thinking his father had returned to say it had all been a horrid mistake. But there was no one there.

Confused, Thaddeus returned his focus to the wall and could hardly believe what he saw. An imp-like shadow was darting between the other shadows, scurrying along like a mouse. It paused next to his mother and cautiously peeled itself from the wall like a piece of old wallpaper, filling out, taking shape. Now Thaddeus could see its shadowy face sniffing the air around his mother.

He gaped. Common sense told him that he was imagining it. Perhaps the coils wrapped around his heart had restricted the blood to his brain and now he was hallucinating. He rubbed his eyes and blinked several times, but the shadow-imp remained. What was more, it was now hunched low, like a cat ready to pounce.

As he watched, it did pounce – right onto

his mother's lap. Thaddeus gasped with disbelief. First pirates, now this!

He shot a startled look at his mother's face, but she showed no indication that she'd felt anything. She remained deeply asleep, her head drooping sideways.

While Thaddeus worried what to do, the shadow-imp seized at a leather strap that hung around its neck. Attached to the strap was a wooden panpipe. The imp lifted the instrument swiftly to its lips and the sweetest music pushed its way into the silent air. The tune was soothing at first, like a beautiful bedtime lullaby, and Thaddeus's body swayed, his eyes became heavy and his head began to nod. Then the music became more forceful and Thaddeus felt a fluttering sensation within his chest, like a bird flexing its wings beneath his ribcage. He snapped awake and the fluttering beneath his ribcage stilled immediately.

He drew in a deep breath and looked at his mother. Her chest was glowing beneath the fabric of her shirt, and the shadow-imp was bending closer to her and playing a more enticing tune. As Thaddeus watched, the glow flickered like the flames of a dozen candles, and then a silvery net, as fine as a spider's web, appeared from the shadow-imp's pocket. It floated into the air and hovered above Thaddeus's mother and the shadow-imp, as if a spider had spun it there. The brightness in his mother's chest increased and suddenly the light streamed out of her and into the air like a cloud of sparkling fireflies. Up, up, up into the air they swirled, dancing around her head until one by one they were caught within the gossamer net.

Thaddeus watched, mesmerised. It was beautiful.

A jubilant smile sprang across the imp's face. It let its panpipe fall back against its chest and carefully gathered the four corners of the net and folded them gently together. Then, lightning-quick, it scampered back along the wall, melted through the window and out onto the front porch.

Thaddeus gasped and turned to his mother. 'Did you feel …? Did you see …?'

One look answered his questions. She hadn't felt or noticed anything. She was still asleep, her only movements the gentle rise and fall of her chest and the tears that seeped from beneath her closed lids.

But as he stared at her more closely, Thaddeus decided there was something different about his mother. She seemed a little more bent, a little more lost, a little more … something he couldn't quite pinpoint.

One thing he was certain of: a filthy, thieving shadow had snatched something from his mother, and on the very same day his father had walked out for good. Well, Thaddeus wasn't about to let the shadowy thief get away with it. He hadn't been able to stop his father leaving, but he could stop an imp from taking what didn't belong to it.

Thaddeus left his mother sleeping silently on the sofa and tore out of the living room, down the hall and out through the front door after the thief.

CHAPTER TWO

MOTHER'S DREAMS

The shadow-imp was hopping around joyfully on the front porch, celebrating what it had taken from Thaddeus's mother. It held the silvery net up to its eyes, then clutched it lovingly to its chest. 'Such lovely things, such treasured things,' it crooned, before hopping off the porch and skipping across the lawn, the trapped fireflies cradled in its arms like a baby.

Thaddeus darted across the lawn after the shadow-imp and tackled it on the driveway.

'What have you got there then?' he said, puffing as he grappled with the net clutched tight in its thieving little mitts.

The net felt soft and sticky like fairy floss, and the flickering fireflies trapped inside warmed his hands like the embers from a fire on a cold day, but that was nothing compared to the feelings that were coming from it. Happiness flowed through Thaddeus, and something else too, something good that he couldn't quite make up his mind about.

It didn't matter – whatever it was that the imp had taken, it belonged to his mother and Thaddeus wasn't about to see her lose something else today.

'It's not yours, you thieving little maggot. Give it back.'

He tried tugging the net out of the shadowy hands, but the imp was surprisingly strong for something so small and it snatched the shimmery square back, before whacking Thaddeus over the head with its free hand.

'Ouch!' Thaddeus fell to the ground, grabbing his head. The imp's hand was as hard as a basketball and the walloping had almost made him see stars. 'But what is it?' he asked dazedly as the shadow-imp held the net closer to its chest.

The imp danced a demented jig around him. 'It's mine! All mine. I sneaked through the crack and I snatched it so it's mine. It's wonderful, it's beautiful, it's Mother's dreams!'

And it flitted away down the drive, caressing and crooning over the silvery net as if it were a precious gem.

'Mother's dreams? And what crack?' wondered Thaddeus, getting slowly to his feet and rubbing his head.

He returned to the porch and looked through the living room window. His mother was still sleeping soundly on the sofa. With her slumped body she looked lost, like … like … Thaddeus thought hard through the pain swelling in his throbbing head … *like all her hopes have been snatched from her all at once.*

That was it! The other feeling that he hadn't quite been able to name when he'd touched the silvery net holding the flickering dreams. It was hope. That manky, stinking imp had stolen his mother's dreams and along with them all her hopes.

Thaddeus spun around and ran after the thieving shadow. He didn't know what a life without dreams might be like, but he knew for certain that a life without hope couldn't be a good thing. He had to get back his mother's dreams and hopes before anything else in their lives could be fixed.

He chased the shadow-imp down the street, following the echo of its shrill voice snickering and muttering jubilantly as it hugged its stolen goods protectively to its chest. He took a short cut across the park, never letting the imp out of his sight. It must have realised it was being chased for it suddenly slung a string of curses over its shoulder and sped up.

Thaddeus ran faster, ignoring the shooting pain that spiralled up from his stomach and pushed like a splinter into his chest. He sprinted past the creek, along the path and across Fowling Road. He didn't stop until he crossed the bridge on High Street, where the lack of oxygen forced him to stop, put his hands on his knees and wheeze for a moment.

It was then that the shadow-imp lost him.

Thaddeus swallowed great gulps of air that burnt all the way down his throat and squeezed his lungs. He cursed himself – why had he stopped? He ran back across the bridge, looking this way and that. Panic set up camp within his still throbbing head. Where would a thieving shadow-imp go?

Thaddeus spied two huge willow trees standing on the bank of the river, their waterfall of leaves keeping secret places hidden. He left the path and crept down the riverbank and quietly pushed beneath the green curtain. The air was softer and cooler here, and the only noises were the whispering of the wind as it tickled the willows' leaves and the occasional chirrup of crickets as they cleared their throats ready for their evening chorus. Thaddeus stood still. If there was magic about, it would surely be here beneath the veil of leaves.

He sensed a movement and turned slowly. There, crouched at the foot of one of the willows, was a large grey cat – *the exact colour of a shadow.*

Thaddeus stared and the cat stared back, its large green eyes never leaving his face. Thaddeus smiled inwardly. He'd read books about witches who could turn into cats so he knew what tricksy things might be disguised within that grey form.

The smile reached his lips right at the same time that he pounced. 'Gotcha!' he said, grabbing hold of the nearest part of the startled cat – its tail.

The cat let out an enraged yowl and swiped Thaddeus viciously across his cheek with a very sharp set of claws. Thaddeus yelped like a wounded puppy and instantly let go of the tail.

'Blasted cat,' he growled, wiping at the bleeding wound with his hand.

The cat commenced cleaning the skin off its claws while watching Thaddeus suspiciously from the corner of its eye.

Thaddeus wasn't entirely convinced that the

cat wasn't hiding a thief, so he tried another tactic. Crouching low, he held out his hand and said, 'Here, kitty, kitty, kitty.'

The cat yawned and, clearly deciding that Thaddeus had learnt his lesson, slouched towards him, rubbed its body against the side of his bent leg and began purring. Thaddeus stood up, pushing the animal away in disgust. There was nothing magical about this particular cat.

He stomped out from beneath the willows' curtaining arms and ran back over the bridge and along High Street. It was getting late and the real shadows were growing long, merging together as the sun sank low in the sky. He knew that once the shadows merged completely into dusk, all would be lost. The shadow-imp would disappear with the night and his mother's dreams would be gone forever.

What was he going to do? He couldn't go home, not without his mother's dreams and hopes. He started to imagine where he might go if he were a thieving magical shadow … but that was just it – he wasn't and so he had no idea. Thaddeus felt a black cloak of despair settle on his shoulders, and it got heavier with each step he took.

He reached the end of High Street and entered a narrow alleyway between two fences that bordered the back of the housing estate. The alley led to an old train line that was only used on Sundays when people paid to ride to the coast in carriages pulled by a steam engine.

He jumped the flimsy wire fence and stumbled across the pebbles that bordered the railway's two steel tracks. He had walked along here many times before and took a moment to breathe in the familiar smells of old coal and warm metal rails.

Nearby, a streetlamp flickered on and Thaddeus blinked. He was too late. Night had moved in. He'd lost the shadow-imp and along with it his mother's dreams. Defeated, he climbed back over the fence.

A twinkling star appeared in the night sky, and the evening wind puffed gently, cooling his warm cheeks. The crickets began their happy chorus. Thaddeus tried to block his ears against them but their chirruping still got through. The noise wasn't helping his throbbing head, and to top it off his heart was really, seriously, aching.

He slumped to sit on the edge of the pavement and wrapped his arms about his chest.

'Aaaaggghh! What am I going to do?' he yelled into the crisp night air.

When no answer came he buried his face in his folded arms and felt fat tears work their way out of his eyes. He rubbed at them angrily before standing up and making his way back home.

He got as far as the bridge on High Street when something sprang out at him.

'Gotcha!'

Thaddeus found himself on the ground with two hairy arms encircling his body like the tongue of a toad strangling a small insect. He looked up and saw that he was completely surrounded by the stinking pirates he'd come face to face with earlier.

'Get off me or I'll scream for the coppers!' he yelled, but a whiffy hand clamped down hard over his mouth and he was pulled roughly to his feet.

'We got 'ims, Silver,' said an exultant voice inches from Thaddeus's ear.

Thaddeus squirmed and bucked within his jailer's grasp. They might have him, but he wasn't going to make it easy for them.

'Gag 'im and put 'im in the sack, me hearties,' ordered Silver.

Not waiting to be told twice, one of the pirates bound Thaddeus's hands behind his back while another roughly gagged him. Then, with the help of the third, they struggled to stuff him into a hessian sack.

'Still got some life in 'im yet,' grunted one.

'I'm gonna bang 'im on the head iffen he don't keep still!'

'No, you don't,' warned Silver. 'We bain't be harmin' a hair on his head, remember? We needs 'im alive to guide us to Pepperjack. After that, we can feed 'im to the fishes.'

The pirates let out bloodthirsty laughs and, with a final heave, Thaddeus was in the sack, which was then thrown roughly over someone's shoulder.

Thaddeus slumped helplessly in his bonds and felt hot tears prick his eyes again. Everything was going wrong. How was he going to get back his mother's dreams now? He might never even see her again.

He bit down hard on the gag and blinked his eyes fiercely, determined not to give in to the tears. He told himself it didn't matter. He comforted himself with the knowledge that he'd escaped from the pirates once, which meant he could escape from them again. It would just be a matter of timing.

Heartened by this thought, Thaddeus bounced and jiggled as much as he could within the confined space of the sack, and was rewarded with a lot of unhappy grunts from the pirate carrying him.

CHAPTER THREE

THE WIZARD ON THE WYDDAH

When Thaddeus got tired of bouncing around, he settled into a somewhat uncomfortable position with his legs crossed and thought about all he'd heard the pirates say. They needed him to lead them to this Captain Pepperjack. Well, they were in for a shock because he didn't know anyone called Pepperjack, let alone where to find him. He wondered what the pirates would do to him when they found this out. Would they take him back to where they'd found him? Or would they do something worse? It was bound to be something worse. Pirates were notorious for doing something worse!

After that, we can feed 'im to the fishes ...

These horrible thoughts were interrupted by the sound of distant thunder. Thaddeus paused in his worrying and concentrated on the noise. Not thunder … waves crashing onto a beach. He felt a chill start at the base of his spine and work its way up to his head. They were taking him to their ugly ship. And that meant he'd be way too close to the ocean. He didn't like the thought of that at all.

He frantically wriggled against his bonds, terror filling every part of him as he remembered that horrible experience of almost drowning.

He was five and he'd gone to the beach with his father, who was fishing off the rocks. Thaddeus had taken his bucket and was busy scouring the little dips in the rocks for any treasures that might have been trapped there after the last tide. He had been so focused on looking down at the rocks that he'd stepped backwards, right off the edge, and toppled into the sea. The current was strong , he didn't know how to swim and the water had immediately covered his head. He remembered the burning in his lungs, the water pressing down on him and darkness all around. He'd tried to claw his way to the surface, but it was impossible in such deep water. Luckily for him, another fisherman saw what had happened and raised the alarm. Thaddeus's father jumped in and fished him to the surface, and kept him afloat until the lifesavers arrived and helped them both back to shore. Thaddeus had never gone in the water again, not even a swimming pool. And because of that, he'd never learnt to swim.

The thundering sound grew louder, and he could taste salty air now through the weave of the hessian. The pirates picked up their pace, and pretty soon Thaddeus heard their feet crunching across sand.

'Signal the *Wyddah*,' Silver ordered.

Thaddeus heard the scratch of a match and saw a blinking glow through the sack – presumably a candle inside a lantern – before a hefty breath doused the signal and plunged them all back into darkness.

'Get the lad out,' said Silver. 'We don't want 'im chokin' on his own stomach like the other one. A bit of fresh air is the best remedy 'til he gets 'ims sea legs.'

Thaddeus barely had time to uncross his legs before he was tumbled roughly onto the sand like a sack of mouldy potatoes.

'Easy now, we don't want 'im bruised,' cautioned Silver, ripping the gag from Thaddeus's mouth.

'Bit late for that,' muttered Thaddeus, standing on shaky legs. 'Just wait till I tell your Captain Pepperjack.'

Silver laughed. 'Best be holdin' yer tongue, little matey, or I'll be 'aving ol' Booth here slappin' that gag back in yer gob.'

Amid the slap of the waves, a scrape was heard.

'Longboat be here,' informed one of the pirates.

'Henry, put the lad in the boat,' Silver said, motioning to the brute who had carried Thaddeus in the sack.

The pirate hoisted Thaddeus over his shoulder and strode into the frothy waves. He threw him into the back of the longboat, between four more pirates who had hold of the oars, and clambered in quickly after him, as if afraid Thaddeus would escape his bonds and make a swim for it. He needn't have worried. Even if Thaddeus didn't have thick rope around his feet, he wouldn't have moved an inch.

With four pirates rowing, it wasn't long until they reached their destination. Thaddeus stared up at the large wooden ship bobbing on the waves, her sails fluttering in the breeze like giant moths' wings.

'Easy there, lads,' said Silver. He stood up, balancing with amazing agility as the longboat bumped against the prow of the ship. 'You first,

Henry, with the boy.'

One of Silver's men lit the lantern again and Thaddeus saw a worn rope ladder dangling down the side of the great groaning hull. Henry slung him again over his ape-like shoulder like a flimsy scarf, and began to climb. Thaddeus felt sick when he realised Henry wasn't holding him at all. Instead, he was using both hands to grasp the rope ladder. He sucked in a worried breath and watched the blackness of the ocean below. Were those frothy tips of the waves reaching for him?

He closed his eyes and tried to pretend he was anywhere but here, but he couldn't shake off the image of his tied-up body dropping into the black sea and sinking like a heavy anchor to the ocean floor. He shivered and tried his best to convince himself that he wasn't scared, just cold from the salt spray dampening his clothes.

It took Henry less than a minute to climb the ladder, but to Thaddeus it was the longest minute of his life. There was a terrifying moment of suspension when Henry paused at the top and waited for two strong hands to grab Thaddeus and pull him over onto the creaking deck. Thaddeus was so relieved to be on a solid footing that he almost couldn't stand. He leant against a nearby barrel and, on wobbly legs, watched the pirates cluster around him like ants to a crumb. They were a smelly, toothless lot, with ragged clothes and bare dirty feet.

Thaddeus focused on one in particular who kept his distance. He had a stump where his hand should have been, and a small chest chained to his other wrist, which he cradled protectively within his arms. He stood alone, and the other pirates didn't seem to notice him as they crowded around Thaddeus, jeering and chattering. Thaddeus felt uncomfortably like an animal in the zoo.

'So you found him.'

The voice was smooth and authoritative, like a headmaster's, and came from behind the clustered pirates. They parted as if swept to each side by an unseen hand, and a man in long emerald-coloured robes marched between them. The pirates tripped over each other as they squashed back as much as possible from the man, their fearful eyes never leaving his cloaked form.

Thaddeus thought it strange that such a fearsome bunch should be afraid of an unarmed man. Well, all except Booth.

He pushed his way to the front of the crowd, his face contorted into an angry scowl.

'No thanks to ye,' he spat at the robed man. 'Just grab 'im, you said. Well, it were poor advice.

'Ims had a fast bike, didn't he?' Booth turned to Silver, who had just negotiated the rope ladder and landed on the deck with a thump. 'I be warning ye, Silver, we should never be trustin' a wizard.'

A flash like lightning momentarily lit up the night sky. Thaddeus saw that the wizard had raised a wand clenched firmly in a bandaged hand. Booth fell to his knees, clutching at his strangled throat.

'*My* magic never fails me, Booth. I advised you to find three children to guide you to Pepperjack and so far you have found two, have you not?'

The wizard flicked his wrist and the invisible cords around Booth's neck tightened. Booth's eyes bulged and his face quickly coloured to an unhealthy shade of blue.

The other pirates all but fell overboard in another effort to distance themselves further from the wizard. Thaddeus now understood the reason for their fear and pushed himself backwards with them.

The wizard paced slowly around the gasping Booth, tapping his wand against the palm of his hand.

'Do you want to know what I think?' he said. 'I think there are some pirates that are just a tad slower than others … hmmm?'

'Now, now, Noxious.' Silver's words shivered

nervously in the cold night air. 'Booth didn't be meanin' it was your fault. He just be frustrated like. The lad seemed to be expectin' us and wouldn't let us anywhere near 'im.'

Thaddeus snickered at Silver's lies. He couldn't help it. After all, he knew very well what had happened. He had been too quick and too smart for these stinking men.

The snicker diverted the wizard's attention and his steely eyes focused on Thaddeus. 'You think it's funny, boy?'

He flicked his wrist and released Booth, who fell on his face and drew in noisy gulps of air. The wizard's wand pointed straight at Thaddeus.

'*Suspendo*!' he snapped.

'No! I –' Thaddeus felt his feet leave the deck and found himself bobbing upside down in front of the foul wizard.

The pirates clearly liked this better than Booth's strangulation. They edged closer, forcing Noxious to move his catch closer to the *Wyddah*'s rails. Although from Thaddeus's point of view, this had seemed to be the wizard's intention all along.

Thaddeus felt a lump form in his throat. He was completely defenceless and at the mercy of a maniac. He tried to wriggle, but his body was limp and weightless. He was a puppet on the end of Noxious's string. All he could do was hang there in frozen terror, listening to the hungry call of the waves that awaited him in the darkness below.

'Spin 'im, Noxious, spin 'im!' called a toothless, dirty-faced crew member. He reached up to spin Thaddeus's body himself, but only succeeded in pushing him further out, right over the rail.

Thaddeus looked down and was almost sick. All he could see were the frothy waves' hungry white-flecked fingers reaching up for him. Panic seized him and his words came out in a garbled mess. 'Put me back, put me back, I didn't mean it, I wasn't laughing!'

'Oh, what have we here? Someone who's afraid of the water?' Noxious laughed, his malice reflected in his eyes as he flicked his wrist.

Thaddeus plummeted towards the waves. His breath left him, his body prickled with fear and all he could hear was the pounding of his heart in his ears. He felt his hair skim the waves before he was lifted back up by Noxious's invisible strings and held level with the mad wizard's eyes.

'Now, now, Noxious, let's be puttin' the lad back on deck,' Silver said. 'You know we be needin' 'im to help us find the Captain. We be livin' a cursed existence without 'im.'

Silver's voice was shaky, and even through Thaddeus's terror he could see that he wasn't the only one sweating. In fact, the sweats seemed contagious, for not only were Silver and the crew affected but great big drops were forming on the wizard's contorted features too. The sight took Thaddeus's mind momentarily off his own predicament. The wizard seemed to be struggling, as if he were holding a heavy load that was causing him great pain.

Then Thaddeus noticed Noxious's wand hand. The clean bandages were no longer white. They were red with blood. And the fingers that gripped the wand were trembling from the pain that seemed to be spreading up the wizard's arm.

'PUT ME DOWN!' screamed Thaddeus.

Noxious paled and his body swayed once before his bleeding hand dropped the wand.

Silver leapt to the edge of the rail, but he was too late. Thaddeus's body no longer hung in the air. It was falling towards the ocean's dark depths.

'AFTER 'IM!' screamed Silver.

***

Thaddeus closed his eyes as his body sliced through the choppy waves. He had gone past panic, past terror, and was now in a place where he was blankly detached. His mind didn't register the three other splashes beside him, nor the strong arms that swept him up above the waves. He didn't notice the strain of wet bodies struggling up the rope ladder, or feel them dragging him back over the *Wyddah*'s rail where they collapsed exhaustedly on the deck.

'Is he dead?' asked someone, nudging Thaddeus's limp body with his bare foot.

'Stand back, ye filthy rats,' blustered Silver. He draped a smelly blanket over Thaddeus and began rubbing life back into his numb limbs.

Thaddeus opened his eyes to see Noxious crouched on the deck cradling his bleeding hand. Anger surged through him, warming him better than any blanket.

He glared furiously at the injured wizard. 'Serves you right, you stinking pig!'

Silver breathed a sigh of relief that he immediately hid in a flurry of orders. 'Raise the anchor!' he yelled. 'Prepare the sails!'

The crew scurried to do his bidding.

'Where to now, Noxious?' asked Silver.

The wizard was still crouched in pain on the deck. 'Safe Harbour,' he said through clenched teeth then stood, hunched over, cradling his hand.

Thaddeus had no doubt that, injured or not, the wizard was still dangerous. Thankfully, Noxious spun on his heel and disappeared down the ship's hatch.

'Make for Safe Harbour,' Silver ordered a pirate with a parrot perched on his shoulder.

Without speaking, the pirate turned and headed for the ship's wheel.

Booth said angrily to Silver, 'Ye be lettin' the wizard get away with that? He almost lost us the boy!'

Silver withdrew his pistol from his belt and took a determined step towards Booth. 'I suggest ye not be forgettin' who be in charge while the Captain's away.'

His words were silky but the threat was sharper than the point of a dagger. Booth backed down immediately.

'Just as I thought,' said Silver, smiling and holstering his pistol. 'Now ye and Henry show the lad to 'ims room!' And he disappeared along the length of the deck, shouting orders.

'Bests untie him,' Booth told Henry, eyeing Thaddeus's ankles and wrists.

While Henry unfastened the ropes, Thaddeus wondered about his options. He didn't have many. Even if he made a run for it, there couldn't be too many hiding places aboard a ship. Especially not one that carried a crazy wizard. He would just have to wait. As soon as the *Wyddah* docked at Safe Harbour, he'd make his move.

This settled, he obeyed Henry's prod in his back and followed Booth to the far end of the *Wyddah*'s deck. There, tied to a mast, was an old wooden chest the size of a very small coffee table. Booth opened the lid and pointed inside.

'Your quarters, lad!' he said with a gummy grin.

Thaddeus blinked at the chest in confusion. Surely they didn't mean to shove him inside it? He wasn't about to exchange one prison for another.

'I'm not going in there!' he said defiantly.

'Oh! 'Ims ain't goin' in there,' mimicked Booth. 'Chuck 'im in, Henry, we doesn't 'ave all night.'

Henry seized Thaddeus like he was a rag doll and threw him into the chest.

CHAPTER FOUR

THE SEA CHEST OF TIMOTHY CLEGG

From the outside it was just an ordinary-sized chest. Inside, however, Thaddeus bounced painfully down six wooden steps and landed on the floor of a sizeable room. He groaned and wondered how many fresh bruises he'd find in the morning.

Standing slowly, he massaged his aching arms and legs and eyed his quarters. They weren't so miserable. By the light of several flickering lanterns hanging along the walls, he noted that the perimeter of the inside of the chest was about the same as his own backyard. It smelt like fresh sea air and old driftwood, and three hammocks hung from its centre beams. Thaddeus got a shock when he noticed one of them wasn't empty.

'So they found you? Welcome aboard the

Black Wyddah.'

The voice belonged to a roly-poly boy with pale skin and tidy blond hair. He was wearing a posh school uniform that looked like it would have cost more than a small car.

'Who was it who found you?' asked the boy. 'Was it Snitch? He's the one who found me. Went off to tell Dibbers and before I knew it, I was in a sack.'

'Snitch?' Thaddeus had no idea what the boy was talking about.

'The parrot – if you can call that mangy scrap of a thing a parrot. He sits on Dibbers' shoulder, looks like he's stitched on. Every time I see him, that's where he is – snitching to Dibbers! The pair of them never miss a thing. They're Silver's eyes and ears aboard the *Wyddah.'*

Thaddeus didn't get a chance to answer the boy's original question because he bulldozed on.

'You just have to watch out for them, that's all. I must say, you have no idea how much grief you caused them. They had a hard time finding you, until the other morning. Never mind, we'll be off now in search of the other one, I expect. I say, you're awfully scrawny, old chap!' The boy struggled to sit up in the hammock and rummaged around in his pocket. He pulled out a squashed chocolate bar. 'Here, take this. You could use it more than me.' He rubbed his bulging stomach self-consciously.

Thaddeus snatched the chocolate bar and began tearing at its wrapper with his teeth. Then he stopped, suddenly wondering if he could trust this boy. After all, he could be on the pirates' side. They might have put him in the chest to get information out of Thaddeus.

'Who are you? Are you one of them?' he blurted.

'One of them?' The boy chuckled. 'I'm one of you.'

'Prove it,' said Thaddeus, still suspicious.

'I can't,' the boy answered regretfully. 'All I can say is that one minute I was sneaking into the kitchens of my school – you know, to get a midnight snack. And the next I was in a sack being dragged and bumped over the ground by two grunting pirates.'

Thaddeus could well imagine the scene, but was still hesitant to give his trust so freely. After all, no one had proved themselves trustworthy since he'd arrived home from school that day.

'I say, are you going to eat that?' asked the boy, pointing a sausage-like finger at the chocolate bar still clutched in Thaddeus's hand.

Thaddeus broke off half and handed it to the boy, who promptly threw it in his mouth and swallowed it whole.

'Oh, that's a relief. I thought it might have been poisoned,' said Thaddeus. He followed the boy's lead and threw the remaining half into his own mouth.

The boy laughed. 'I'm Juniper, Juniper Rose.'

He held out his pudgy hand and shook Thaddeus's as if it were a twig that might break.

'Thaddeus Bix,' said Thaddeus, unsure whether Juniper might already know his name. It seemed he didn't. 'What is this place?'

The room looked like ten jumble sales all crammed together, with clutter piled higgledy-piggledy against the walls and threatening to topple with each rock of the ship.

'Asked myself the same thing when they first brought me aboard,' Juniper said. 'That was weeks ago now. They emptied my pockets and took everything I had. Lucky for me that I don't just keep chocolate bars in my pocket. Stupid pirates didn't think to check anywhere else.' He laughed sheepishly. 'Still, I'm glad they're stupid or they might have gotten my charm.'

He tugged at a chain around his neck and pulled out a small charm with a dull insignia on the front. Thaddeus thought it looked like a piece of junk.

'What is it?' he asked.

'Not a clue, old chap, but it's one of the last things my parents gave me. Now it's the only thing I have to remind me of them,' said Juniper sadly.

'Are your parents dead?'

Juniper shook his head. 'Not dead, but I haven't seen them in over a year. They're on a dig somewhere – they're archaeologists, you know. Anyway, after the pirates emptied my pockets I didn't know if I'd be left here to starve, so I searched this entire room … er, chest … for food.'

'Did you find anything?' asked Thaddeus eagerly.

'No – not food at any rate. But I did find out that this sea chest must have once belonged to someone called Timothy Clegg. A sea chest is what a sailor takes aboard a ship to carry all his belongings, only this one's not your normal sort. It's magic. I'm thinking it was made by a wizard. See the inscription over there – it reads *Zelba's Room To Move.*'

Juniper pointed to a brass plate half-obscured by a box. Thaddeus moved closer to look, but was instantly distracted by the contents of the box. He found a broken compass, several decks of cards, a stuffed monkey with eerie eyes that seemed to follow him no matter where he stood, and a hand mirror that looked like it belonged to a girl.

'Not the sort of thing you'd think a sailor would own,' he said to Juniper as he held it up to his face.

To Thaddeus's astonishment, the reflection wasn't his own. It was of a grumpy-faced man wizened with age. He promptly blew a raspberry at Thaddeus before shouting, 'You're so ugly you crack me up.' Then the mirror cracked.

'Not very nice, is he?' said Juniper, heaving himself out of his hammock and coming to stand beside Thaddeus.

Thaddeus picked up a rolled piece of parchment. 'I wonder what this is.'

Juniper shrugged. 'I didn't bother unrolling it. I mean, it's not like there could be food hidden inside it.'

'But it could be a treasure map,' said Thaddeus, quickly unrolling the scroll. 'It's a contract,' he said, disappointed, 'between William Booth and Captain Tyran Pepperjack.'

'I say – is that blood?' asked Juniper, pointing to the squiggle of Booth's signature.

'I think so – it'd make sense. Look at what it says: *I, William Booth, do swear on my life's blood to faithfully serve Captain Tyran Pepperjack* – look at the list of clauses! It says at the end that Booth can't be freed from this contract unless he or the Captain dies.'

Thaddeus snorted and stuffed the scroll back into the box. 'You'd have to be an idiot to sign your name to something like that. I wonder what something of Booth's is doing in Clegg's sea chest?'

'I don't know, old chap, but I've found a few things belonging to Booth. Maybe they were friends.'

Thaddeus opened a little leather notebook titled *The Art of Knotting*. Immediately a piece of rope and diagrams appeared on the notebook's blank page. Thaddeus put down the book where he could see the diagrams, picked up the rope and followed each step.

'It's not that hard,' he said to Juniper as he tied the last loop.

Juniper looked at the knot doubtfully. 'It doesn't look quite the same, old chap.'

The notebook didn't think so either, because the diagrams dissolved and a single sentence appeared: *Not like that, you idiot!* The book snapped shut and the piece of rope disappeared from Thaddeus's hand. Thaddeus kicked the box against the wall in disgust.

'I couldn't manage it either,' said Juniper consolingly before changing the subject. 'I say, did you see Noxious on deck? I don't think I'd like to mess with him, especially not after what he did to poor old Timothy Clegg.'

Thaddeus's face turned red at the mention of the wizard. He didn't want Juniper to know what had happened to him only moments before. He moved out of the other boy's line of sight and began prowling about the sea chest. There was a heavy cupboard in the back corner and he grasped its handle.

'I wouldn't open that if I were you,' said Juniper.

'Why not?'

'It has a skeleton inside.'

'A skeleton? Whose – Timothy Clegg's?'

Thaddeus's tone was sarcastic, but Juniper seemed oblivious.

'I don't know that it's Clegg's, but I do know that I made the mistake of opening that cupboard the first night they dumped me in here. It was rattling ever so loudly and … well, to me it sounded like a bunch of chefs clattering pots and pans in a kitchen. If a chest can become a room, why can't a cupboard become a kitchen?

I never thought it would hold a skeleton. It took me ages to chase it back inside.' He shuddered at the memory.

Thaddeus moved away from the cupboard, deciding to take Juniper's word for it.

'So who is this Clegg anyway?' he asked, letting his eyes wander further along the wall to what looked suspiciously like a rubbish tip in the far corner. The pile held an assortment of old clothing, piles of leathery books, bits of frayed rope, and shredded sails and other seafaring paraphernalia. There was one thing Thaddeus knew for sure – Timothy Clegg had been a hoarder.

'Well, that's just it, I don't know exactly who he was. I only know what I've watched in his memoir,' answered Juniper.

Thaddeus had moved past the messy pile and was inspecting the shelves of a heavy bookcase. 'Watched? Don't you mean you read his memoir?'

Juniper opened his mouth to answer, but was cut off by a loud grinding, clanking sound.

'The anchor,' he explained in response to Thaddeus's questioning look. 'Now where was I … oh, yes, the memoir …'

He reached into his hammock and pulled out a fat leather volume that looked very old and very worn. The kind of book you might find in a dusty old antiques store.

'*This* is Clegg's memoir. It's a living book,' Juniper said, his eyes sparkling with excitement as he handed it to Thaddeus. 'Here, see for yourself. I've never seen anything like it. Of course, you wouldn't in our world because no one believes in magic any more. But that doesn't mean it's not there, does it?'

Thaddeus hadn't believed in magic. But that was before he'd seen a shadow-imp steal his mother's dreams and hopes, and got kidnapped by a bunch of filthy pirates and thrown into a sea chest whose inside was way bigger than its outside.

Juniper heaved himself back into his hammock. 'My parents told me to always believe in the unseen. It's why they're good at what they do. They have no proof that there are treasures below the surface, but they believe they're there, they search for them, and most often than not they're rewarded.'

Thaddeus nodded. He decided to tell Juniper about the shadow-imp stealing his mother's dreams, which was what had landed him in this predicament.

'It's the same as your parents said,' he finished. 'I never actually saw my mum's dreams before the shadow-imp stole them, but that doesn't mean they didn't exist. They were real, and now they've gone. It was weird, you know – right at the moment I saw the imp on the wall, time seemed to stop and my mum fell into this weird sleep.' He looked down at the memoir and fiddled with the corner of its cover. 'She'll be all alone. My dad left, and now I'm gone too …'

'I'm awfully sorry to hear that, old chap. If it's any consolation, my father always says that what is lost can be found again. I'd say that includes everything, even dreams. We'll get them back for her, you see if we don't. As for her being all alone, maybe the shadow-imp cast a spell over her – you know, like in a fairytale – and she'll stay asleep until you bring her dreams back.'

Thaddeus was silent for a moment, thinking over Juniper's suggestion. But he'd have to escape the pirates first before he could go searching for his mother's dreams.

'How do you suppose they think we're going to help them find their Captain?' he asked.

'I overheard Booth and Henry talking about kidnapping three children – that's us, I guess, and whoever else they're off to find now. I don't know why though.'

'Why don't they just make someone else their

Captain?'

'Well, they're bound to Pepperjack by contract, aren't they. You saw that scroll – only death can free them. Pepperjack must be imprisoned somewhere. Still, I certainly wouldn't want him to come back – he's blooming awful!'

Thaddeus's eyes almost hopped out of his head, 'Have you seen him? How … when?'

Juniper pointed a sausage finger at the memoir that was still in Thaddeus's hands. 'He's in there, and he's not nice. Go on – open it and see for yourself.'

Thaddeus opened the book and immediately felt a spray of cold sea on his hand. The feeling was the same as if a spider had just darted across his skin and he dropped the book in shock.

'I say, old chap, it's just a little bit of ocean,' said Juniper, stretching out of his hammock to pick the memoir up off the floor.

'I've just had enough of the ocean for one night,' Thaddeus explained, and he told Juniper about his cold bath and the wizard responsible for it.

'He's a nasty one, that Noxious,' Juniper said. 'Well, that explains why you're all wet. I thought you might have tried to escape and failed. That's why I didn't say anything.'

Thaddeus smiled at Juniper's attempt at tact.

'There are some dry clothes over there,' Juniper added, pointing to a cobwebby pile between the junkyard corner and the overburdened bookcase. 'Go on, you may as well be warm while we look at the memoir.'

Thaddeus quickly tossed aside his wet clothes and found a pair of oversized breeches and a baggy top. More fossicking and the pile gave up a big buckled belt that held the pants up, and a worn jacket the exact shade of the sack that Thaddeus had been shoved into.

Juniper guffawed with laughter. 'Sorry, old chap – but you look just like one of those filthy pirates up there.'

Thaddeus grinned. 'Beggars can't be choosers!'

Juniper bunched himself up awkwardly in the hammock to make room for Thaddeus to squeeze in next to him. Thaddeus pulled Clegg's memoir onto his lap, struggling to make himself comfortable squished against Juniper's round form.

'You should see what that Noxious gets up to in this memoir,' Juniper said. 'He's a wicked piece of work.'

'So what is a memoir anyway? And why is

there sea in it?' asked Thaddeus.

'Like I said before, old chap, it's a living book. Like a diary, but not your usual sort. This one has some missing pages though – here, have a look.'

Juniper opened the memoir, and Thaddeus found himself looking at something like a theatre play, with real-life figures acting out the story.

'That's unbelievable,' he said, enraptured.

The scene showed a rocky island with a few ships at anchor at the end of a long pier. Thaddeus recognised one of them as the *Black Wyddah*. The wind was howling and Thaddeus felt it blowing off the page and tousling his hair. The crew from another ship were battling along the slippery wave-soaked pier, making their way towards the only building on the rocky isle.

'That's Timothy Clegg,' said Juniper, pointing to a man scurrying along in front of the ragged bunch.

At the end of the pier, Clegg leapt up some stone steps to a door beneath a creaking wooden sign that said *The Travelling Bard Inn*. He entered the warmth of the bar room and Thaddeus and Juniper went with him.

Thaddeus took in the room. A vast fire roared in its centre, warming all the circular tables clumped around it. In the corner a skeleton thumped out a tune on a worn piano.

'One pickled rum,' Clegg said, and the clink of a coin drew Thaddeus's eyes towards the bar. Clegg was leaning with his back against it, casually surveying all the tables. His gaze paused on one in a dim corner.

The barkeeper placed a tankard on the counter. It contained a thick black drink that bubbled with froth like churning ocean waves . Clegg picked it up and sauntered over to the corner.

'This seat taken?' he asked, scraping a wooden chair out from the table.

The men looked up and Thaddeus realised they were some of the pirates from the *Wyddah* – Silver, Booth, Henry, and a richly dressed man whose face remained secret beneath the brim of a red plumed hat. Thaddeus peered closer, but no matter what angle he tried, the face remained hidden.

He looked at Juniper. 'Who's that then?'

'Shhh, you're missing it,' Juniper said, his eyes never leaving the memoir.

Frustrated, Thaddeus returned his gaze to the page.

The pirates gulped back their drinks and called for more. In between the barkeeper's rounds, it became clear that Clegg was trying to barter his way onto the *Wyddah*. The crew ignored his requests and began playing cards. They were halfway through their game when another newcomer joined them. Thaddeus recognised the emerald robes immediately.

'Look at his hand – it's not bleeding!' whispered Thaddeus.

'Shhhhh!' said Juniper again.

'Who be this then?' a drunken Clegg asked Booth, who was sitting next to him.

'That be Noxious,' spat Booth, his lips curled into a snarl. 'The Captain's –'

'A wizard?' Clegg exclaimed, then hiccuped. 'Ye let a wizard on the *Wyddah* and not me?' He kicked back his chair and stood, his body swaying clumsily. 'Well, let me be tellin' ye something – *hic* – I be havin' more power than any stinkin' wizard – *hic*!'

His flow of words was interrupted by a noisy belch. Thaddeus and Juniper screwed up their faces as the smell wafted out of the memoir and assaulted their nostrils.

'That's disgusting,' mumbled Thaddeus.

Clegg carried on, oblivious to the two onlookers hovering over him. 'Ye see – *hic* – only I be knowin' where be the most sought-after treasure of all time – *hic*.'

The bar room became instantly silent and all eyes focused on Clegg's smirking, swaying form.

'That's right,' he said. 'Only I be knowin' where the Thureos be hidden!'

A collective gasp seemed to explode around the warm smoky room. The barkeeper dropped the glass he was filling, but nobody took any notice.

Henry snorted. 'Ye be talkin' through yer butt, Clegg. The Thureos be a legend, nothin' more. There be nothin' in this world that can protect a person from death's hand. Nothin'.'

Clegg's face grew red. 'Legends – *hic* – always be founded on truth – *hic* – ye stupid pirate. I be tellin' ye it exists. I seen it and held it in me own hands – *hic* – and felt the protection flowin' from it – *hic*. It be true alright.'

The shadowy figure in the corner seemed to take particular interest in Clegg's words. Thaddeus noticed him leaning forwards, anticipating what was to come. But Clegg had stopped talking. His head slowly slumped towards his chest.

Booth scraped his chair back, stood, grabbed Clegg's arm and shook it. 'Where is it?' he demanded, desperation written all over his face.

But Clegg had given in to the potency of the pickled rum. His eyes rolled back in his head and his face fell flat on the table.

The memoir page became blank.

Thaddeus frowned at Juniper. 'What was that all about? And what's a Thureos?'

Juniper raised his hand as if he were holding a stop sign at a school crossing. 'Steady on, one question at a time. The whole book is full of little scenes like that – I've watched them all. As for the Thureos, I have no idea what it is. It's only mentioned a handful of times in the whole memoir.'

Thaddeus stared. A whole book full of little scenes. It would be better than watching television.

'Well, I have been imprisoned in this chest for two whole weeks,' said Juniper defensively, misinterpreting Thaddeus's stare.

Thaddeus feverishly flicked through the book's other pages. He wanted more. He wanted to find out what happened to Clegg.

'He dies,' said Juniper.

'What?' Thaddeus tore his eyes from a page that showed a market with stalls piled high with colourful pyramids of spices. The aromas wafting out made his stomach grumble. 'What do you mean?'

'Clegg – he dies ... well, he's murdered.'

Juniper said the last word in a whisper and it took a few seconds for its meaning to get from

Thaddeus's ears to his brain. '*Murdered?*'

Juniper nodded sombrely. 'It happens on the last page. Oh, you should watch that part too – it's interesting.'

He pointed at the current page, and Thaddeus looked down to see a new scene playing out.

Clegg and Booth were walking together along a bustling wharf.

Clegg looked worried and repeatedly glanced over his shoulder. 'So what d'ye say, Booth? Are we in agreeance?'

Booth's eyes had the feverish hue of a gold digger's. 'Aye, I agree to be yer heir.'

'Ye be knowin' what it means?'

'Aye, aye,' said Booth impatiently. 'Should somethin' befall ye, I be inheritin' all yer worldly goods.'

'And debts,' said Clegg with emphasis.

'Debts too. Now where do I sign?'

Clegg quickened his pace, seeming eager to leave the wharf behind. He and Booth were soon darting in and out of alleyways, and Booth seemed to be having trouble keeping up. Thaddeus could hear him puffing.'It has to be a bindin' promise,' Clegg said. 'Nothin' else will do. And ye know what that means?'

Booth nodded. 'And I be gettin' *all* yer worldly

goods – includin' the Thureos?'

Clegg smiled, and Thaddeus, watching intently, couldn't help thinking it was a sad smile.

'Ye be gettin' all me worldly possessions, Booth.'

The scene dissolved and a new one started almost immediately on the next page.

Clegg and Booth were now in what looked like an old library. They were standing before a black-robed wizard.

'I have to ask both of you gentlemen formally if you are in agreeance with the contract that is about to take place and all its clauses?' the wizard said.

'Aye, aye!' said Booth impatiently.

The wizard glared at him for a moment before using his wand to summon a strand of hair from each of their heads.

'Would you shake hands, please,' the wizard said.

He flicked his wand, and the two hairs intertwined and wrapped themselves around the joined hands of Clegg and Booth. The wizard mumbled something indecipherable and Clegg and Booth released each other's hand.

Clegg reached into his pocket, produced two silver coins and placed them into the wizard's palm. Then he and Booth left the room.

Thaddeus had to let his eyes readjust as the dimness of the wizard's room was replaced by the brightness of a cobbled street.

Clegg turned to Booth. 'Goodbye, Booth. Be kind to yerself and remember there is never honour amongst thieves.'

A yell cut off Clegg's words. Thaddeus's eyes flicked to the edge of the page to see who was yelling. When he looked back at the memoir, the scene was dissolving. The last thing he saw was Clegg fleeing and Booth staring after him with a grin on his face.

Thaddeus quickly flipped the page – but there was only one more left in the book. In-between were the ragged edges of the torn-out section.

'Oh no! What happened? Who ripped them out?'

'I don't know, I found it like that. But that last page is the awful part, old chap.'

Thaddeus immediately felt hot air emanating off the page before he could see anything. The scene appeared like a mirage, hazy at first before becoming solid.

Clegg was in a dingy room. He was peering anxiously out of a grimy window at a deserted street lit by a straggle of gas lanterns. It was raining and steamy puddles were forming between the cobblestones. It must have been quite late because the moon hung high in the sky.

'He doesn't look well, does he?' Juniper's voice broke through Thaddeus's concentration, making him jump.

Thaddeus nodded, not taking his eyes off Clegg, who did look worse for wear. He was thin and weary, like he'd been on the run for a long time. His face was grey and set in a mask of defeat. Sweat trickled down his forehead and his hands shook each time he lifted back the curtain to peer out into the night.

Suddenly he let out a strangled groan and his eyes flicked from the window to the bed. Thaddeus's gaze followed and he realised there was an old sea chest hidden under it.

'Is that this chest?' he asked Juniper, ducking his head lower for a better look.

'Yes – keep watching, old chap.'

Thaddeus returned his attention to Clegg, whose whole face was now glistening with sweat. He had his back to the window and was facing the bedroom door with both hands raised defensively.

The door crashed open and two figures stood silhouetted in the light from the hall.

Clegg fell to his knees. 'Please … I be beggin' ye!'

The figures stepped into the room and Thaddeus saw a richly dressed pirate wearing a hat with a red plume. He had a jet-black pointed beard, and thick gold hoops hung from his ears. Beside him, wand raised in a neatly bandaged hand, stood Noxious.

The pirate placed his hand over the wand and lowered it to the wizard's side, leaving no one in doubt as to who held the authority in this scene.

'I understand ye be having something I want,' drawled the pirate, walking in a circle around the helpless Clegg. He withdrew a dagger from its sheath at his belt and began picking his nails with it.

'I don't … I can't …' said Clegg. His whole body was quivering and he looked about to collapse.

'Can't, or won't?' the pirate said, stopping behind him.

'Captain Pepperjack … please, I … the Thureos is not mine to give …' Clegg's voice dribbled away and he cowered to the floor.

Thaddeus gasped and almost dropped the memoir. 'That's Pepperjack?' he squeaked, feeling like someone had just doused him with icy water.

Juniper nodded. 'He's frightful, isn't he? Keep watching.'

Captain Pepperjack turned to Noxious and barked, 'Search the room.'

Noxious pointed his wand towards the bed. '*Revelare.*'

The sea chest shot out. At the same time, Clegg sprang into action.

'NO!' he yelled, and lunged for the wizard so fast that he caught him off guard. He grabbed hold of Noxious's wand arm and bit into it, but the wizard shook him off.

'Kill him!' ordered Pepperjack, his gleaming eyes fixed on the trunk at his feet. 'We have what we came for.'

Noxious hesitated, and Thaddeus noticed that the bandage on his hand began to turn red.

'Ye know what happens when ye defy me. It amazes me that still ye do it,' said Pepperjack, his voice steely.

Noxious supported his wand hand with his other and muttered a curse. A flash of light exploded from the wand and hit Clegg squarely in the chest. Clegg fell to the floor, his lifeless eyes seemed to be staring beneath the bed where he'd tried to hide the sea chest.

The scene dissolved and the memoir became

blank again.

Thaddeus almost fell out of the hammock as he spun to face Juniper. 'Did you see that?'

Juniper's hair flopped as he nodded vigorously, but Thaddeus wasn't convinced he understood what he was really saying.

'Jupe, I know you saw it, but did you get it?'

'I say, I'm not daft, you know. I saw exactly what happened. Noxious killed Timothy Clegg. That wizard is a maniac – someone ought to report him.'

'No, not that – the other bit.'

Thaddeus let out a long breath and slowly counted to five while he watched Juniper's vacant expression. How could Juniper not see it? He had obviously watched the scene more than once and its significance was as clear as a summer sky.

'Pepperjack, Jupe!'

'Oh, I know, old chap, he's perfectly horrid. Don't think I'm looking forward to meeting him when the time comes. Still, we'll give him what he wants, then we can go home. I wonder if my school will have a welcome home banquet for me –'

'JUNIPER!' Thaddeus couldn't believe his new friend was so blind.

Juniper crossed his arms protectively over his

chest. 'No need to shout, I'm just here.'

'We won't be going home – not alive anyway.'

'Now you listen here, old chap, why would you say such a horrid thing? Of course we'll be going home.'

'You saw it, Jupe.' Thaddeus pointed to the closed and silent memoir. 'Once Pepperjack gets what he wants, he does away with what he doesn't need any more.'

Inside the sea chest was perfectly quiet now, only the muffled slap of the waves against the *Wyddah*'s moving hull breaking the silence. Thaddeus watched as understanding dawned on Juniper's face, blanching it white.

'What should we do?' he whispered, his voice strangled with fear.

'We have to escape, the first chance we get. I need to find my mother's dreams and get home to her, and you need to find your parents.'

'But how, old chap? We're on a ship full of desperate pirates and a wizard – not to mention that said ship is in the middle of the sea miles from land!'

'I don't know,' answered Thaddeus. 'But I do know what we definitely shouldn't be doing, Juniper. We shouldn't ever be meeting Captain Pepperjack.'

CHAPTER FIVE

SKIP FOWLER

Thaddeus and Juniper remained locked in the sea chest for the next week. Juniper counted off the days against the number of dinners they were served. As far as prisons went, the sea chest wasn't too horrendous. It seemed a Zelba's sea chest was built for comfort, with a toilet and shower that appeared and disappeared as needed, and a dining table that popped up at mealtimes. The boys spent the time getting to know each other, rewatching the scenes in the memoir, and making various plans of escape. They agreed that they wouldn't attempt an escape at sea, as neither fancied trying to outrun the *Black Wyddah* in a small rowboat. Thaddeus was especially opposed to this idea given his lack of swimming ability.

'So it's settled,' he said. 'We make a run for it when the *Wyddah* docks at Safe Harbour. Agreed?'

'Agreed,' said Juniper through a mouthful of dried-out chicken drumstick and squashed peas. He seemed to be paying more attention to the food than he was to Thaddeus. He pointed to the remains of Thaddeus's meal. 'I say, are you going to eat that?'

Thaddeus grimaced and pushed his plate forwards. Juniper fell upon it with the ferocity of a tiger.

'Where do you suppose Pepperjack got to?' Thaddeus asked for what must have been the thousandth time. 'It seems strange that a Captain would abandon his ship.'

Juniper shrugged and scraped up the last of the peas on Thaddeus's plate before picking it up and licking it clean.

'He's probably in prison somewhere,' he said between licks. 'No more than he deserves.'

Thaddeus mulled it over. He didn't think that could be right, or the pirates wouldn't have needed three children to help them find him.

***

On the eighth morning, Thaddeus awoke to the smell of fresh air and the gentle tickle of a breeze upon his cheek. He opened his eyes to see a thick stream of sunlight bouncing off the sea chest's steps. The lid was wide open.

'All hands on deck, old chap,' said Juniper joyfully, poking his head through the opening. His blond hair ruffled and his fleshy cheeks were soon flecked with salt spray.

Thaddeus didn't need to be told twice. He leapt from his hammock, bounded up the steps two at a time, and joined Juniper on the deck.

He'd barely taken two breaths before they were joined by a boy with a round face and spiky hair. He looked very much like the sea urchins that some of the pirates were scraping from the side of the *Wyddah*. The boy handed Thaddeus and Juniper a scrubbing brush each and a wooden pail full of salty water.

Juniper looked at his brush in offence. 'I say, are you new here? I don't think I've seen you about before. And what about this brush? I mean to say, what's a fellow to do with it? Is it a gift? Funny gift … one would usually expect cheese or chocolate or even *breakfast*!'

'Name's Skip, Skip Fowler,' answered the boy cheerily. 'And best ye get on yer knees, Juniper, and start scrubbing before Silver changes 'ims mind and has ye cleaning out the head. He be in an unfriendly mood this morning.' Skip directed his eyes to where Silver was holding a nasty-looking whip in his hand and berating the pirate with the missing arm. 'Silver caught Stubbs without the Captain's memoirs. Stubbs be charged with guarding them memoirs with his life, but he always be trying to unchain himself from 'em, so Silver be punishing him.'

'Is that what's inside that small chest he had chained to him – Pepperjack's memoir? Is it like a play too?' asked Thaddeus a little too eagerly.

Skip looked at him as if he was crazy. 'All memoirs do be the same.'

'I didn't be leavin' them, Silver!' yelled Stubbs. 'It's a trick, I tell ye. I'd be losin' me other arm rather than losin' the Captain's memoirs! I be under a spell!'

But Silver wasn't listening. He raised his whip.

While the rest of the crew jeered at their unfortunate mate, who now lay across the body of a cannon, his back bared, Thaddeus noticed a beefy pirate who stood taller than the rest, his muscled arms folded in satisfied pleasure. He was staring at the one-armed pirate with a smug look that suggested he'd been the cause of this situation. Thaddeus glimpsed a collection of feathers on the beefy pirate's shoulder and realised the pirate must be Dibbers and the feathers must be his parrot, Snitch. Thaddeus didn't like the look of either of them, especially when Dibbers' satisfied expression turned to glee as Silver lashed the cat-o'-nine-tails across Stubbs's bare back.

As if he felt Thaddeus's stare, Dibbers turned and looked him full in the face. The pirate crooned something into his parrot's ear and the mangy bird swivelled its head to look at the three boys, then spread its enormous wings.

'Quick! Start scrubbing,' hissed Skip.

Thaddeus and Juniper instantly fell to their knees and, following Skip's lead, dipped their brushes in the bucket and began scrubbing the deck.

The parrot fluttered over and planted itself on the rigging somewhere above their heads.

'Were you kidnapped too?' Thaddeus asked Skip, trying to ignore the beady bird eyes he felt boring into his back.

Skip grinned. 'No, I be one of the crew. Silver's kept me below decks mending sails since before Juniper arrived. It be me punishment, see.'

'I say, you'll know all about Captain Pepperjack then – what happened to him?' asked Juniper.

'None of us be knowing,' said Skip. 'For years, he be looking for the most sought-after treasure – he be wanting it all for himself – and next thing we knows, he be gone. Disappeared into the darkness of night.'

'Why do you need to find him?' asked Thaddeus. 'Why can't you just leave him where he is and get on with your life? It's what I'd do!'

'At first we did be celebrating his disappearance, 'cause he ain't a nice Captain, but then we realised that we be cursed without him.'

Skip stopped scrubbing and pulled back his hair to reveal his left ear. He pointed to a black smudge the size of a pea on the base of his skull behind the ear. It seemed to be moving. Thaddeus and Juniper leaned in for a closer look.

'I say, is that a tattoo of the *Black Wyddah*?' asked Juniper.

Skip nodded and began scrubbing again. 'When we signed up for the *Wyddah*, we didn't know we was also signing a vow never to be leaving the Captain or his ship. When he disappeared some of us be trying to leave, but that mark appeared and burnt into our brains, reminding us we can't be going anywhere without him. Without the Captain, we don't have no direction or purpose. And without purpose we don't be having any hope. He be our leader and we signed them contracts with our life's blood.'

Thaddeus snorted. 'Pepperjack doesn't sound

like anyone I'd want to be loyal to. Can't someone remove the mark for you?'

'Only the Captain can be setting us free – and the only freedom he be wanting to give us be the one that comes with death. No, we be marked as his for life.'

Skip looked miserable as he scrubbed the deck and Thaddeus couldn't help but feel sorry for him. It still didn't explain how he and Juniper fitted into the pirates' plans though.

'That's awful, Skip. But how are we supposed to find Pepperjack? We've never even met him.'

'Silver – he be second in charge – he asked the wizard straightsaway on how to find the Captain. Noxious be telling us that we be needing to find the lost parts in ourselves to guide us to the Captain – he be calling them "virtues". Silver says he don't even know what a virtue is, so the wizard be explaining that it's something good to guide a person in their life, like a compass. It's most powerful in children, but a pirate can get virtue too, if he's willing to spend years learning it. Silver be impatient so he be asking the wizard how he can steal virtue from a child to guide us to the Captain.'

'What a lazy scheming maniac,' said Thaddeus, moving closer to Skip in order to hear better.

'The wizard be telling Silver that virtue can't be stolen. It's in the heart of a person, and to take the heart would be to kill the person. Silver got boiling mad over that. He be used to taking whatever he wants.'

Thaddeus didn't much like the sound of Silver having to kill a person to get their heart and its virtue. Was that what the pirates were planning to do to him and Juniper?

'Why does he need three of us?' he asked Skip.

'The wizard be saying there's power in three. "By the power of three we may see" – that's what he be telling Silver. Like the moon and stars by night and the sun by day, or the past, present and future of time. Three be a powerful number. So Silver be ordering the wizard to find three children.'

'I say, old chap, you're a child too,' said Juniper. 'Why can't Silver use your virtue as well?'

Skip turned red. 'I be a pirate, that's why. But I be wanting a compass like other children, so ever since I be doing what the wizard told Silver he had to do to learn virtue.' His voice lowered to a whisper and his eyes took on a dreamy glaze. 'When I be looking after her, I be practising my virtue. No one else wants to look after her – they be too afraid.

But I be liking her company, and I do nice things for her so she don't hurt me. She be telling me that soon I'll be getting my own compass.'

Thaddeus and Juniper said in unison, 'Her?'

Skip stopped scrubbing and looked frightened. He flicked a worried glance towards the parrot up in the rigging, then darted his eyes back to the stern where Silver was still whipping the unfortunate Stubbs.

Thaddeus wasn't going to let the slip pass. There were things he wanted to know. 'Her?' he said again.

Skip deftly changed the topic. 'The room where I be mending the sails be right beneath yer chest. I heard every conversation – yer words be sinking right through the floor and into my lap. Ye be scared of the Captain, and ye be plotting and planning to get away. I be hearing it all!'

Skip looked pointedly at Thaddeus and was rewarded with a red blush that Thaddeus felt staining his cheeks. Skip had thrown him off track … for now.

'I say, you won't tell Silver about our plan, will you?' Juniper asked Skip worriedly.

Skip shook his head. 'I ain't like Dibbers and Snitch. I just be keeping me ears open and me gob shut. But I be telling ye something – ye won't be escaping at Safe Harbour. Ye don't know what Silver has planned. He ain't stupid, he –'

'YE NO GOOD SCUM-BUCKET URCHIN!' Silver roared. 'WHY BAIN'T THE DECK BE SWABBED YET? YE BE WANTIN' A TASTE OF THIS TOO?'

He descended on them like an unexpected storm and gave a flick of his wrist, sending the cat-o'-nine-tails snapping like lightning against the deck. Skip went white and dropped his brush. Silver smiled, grabbed Skip by the scruff of his neck and gave him a vicious shake.

Dibbers appeared wearing an eager smile, the parrot on his shoulder again.

'Keelhaul 'im!' squawked Snitch, dancing around excitedly.

Skip whimpered and Juniper looked terrified.

Dibbers rubbed his pockmarked face fondly against the bird's feathers. 'There, there, my pet. All in good time. Silver be knowin' best.'

Thaddeus noted the expectant gaze in the pirate's bloodshot eyes and knew that Dibbers would be barracking for Snitch's idea of dragging Skip underneath the ship from bow to stern. But Dibbers' words had the opposite effect on Silver.

He puffed out his chest like a strutting rooster and said, 'Ye be right, Dibbers – I does be knowin' best. That's why Captain Pepperjack be leavin' me in charge.'

And he released Skip so fast that the boy plunged backside first into the pail of water.

Disappointed, Dibbers and Snitch moved off in search of fresh mischief.

Thaddeus didn't like the way Silver had treated Skip. He leaned close to Juniper and said in a deliberately loud voice, 'Pepperjack can't be that smart if he left Silver in charge.'

Silver's eyes narrowed. 'Ye'd be wise to watch yer tongue, Bix. These winds can carry words far and wide. I wouldn't be in yer shoes iffen the Captain were to catch yer words in his ears. And it won't be long now. All we be needin' is the last child. I be hearin' that virtue callin' to us like the thunder calls the rains. And I be telling ye somethin' for nothin', me hearty – it'll be ye who gets it for me.' He stabbed his dirty finger into Thaddeus's chest.

'I'd like to see you make me,' snorted Thaddeus, his nerve returning. 'Don't think I'm gonna help you bring back some stinking thieving pirate who might kill me on sight!'

Silver gave an evil grin. 'I thoughts ye might be sayin' that. So I be givin' ye a choice. Either ye can get the last child, or he can.' He pointed at

Juniper. 'But I be tellin' ye this, the one that stays behind will be goin' for a swim should the other not return. And where ye be goin' to get the last child, there be plenty of food.'

Thaddeus didn't have to look at Juniper's hungry eyes to know that, plan or no plan, he didn't trust Juniper to come back for him. Not if there was food involved.

'What do you want me to do?' he asked Silver with sudden meekness.

The little pirate swelled like a bullfrog on a lily pad. 'That be more like it,' he croaked. 'Now swab the deck, me hearties, and make sure ye be swabbin' it good.' He lifted his peg leg and booted Skip across the arm with it. 'As for ye, ye no good scurvy dog, ye best be gettin' the lads their breakfast.'

Skip tore off across the deck faster than a musket-fired ball. Silver laughed heartily, missing the angry tint spreading across Thaddeus's face. Thaddeus dropped his own scrubbing brush and stood. He was taller than Skip by a foot, which made him the same height as Silver.

'Why don't you pick on someone your own size?' he said.

Silver's laugh rumbled to a dead stop. He looked menacingly at Thaddeus. 'Someone else be wantin' a taste of me peg?' he said silkily, and raised the wooden leg with intent.

Thaddeus didn't think twice. He grabbed the end of the leg and yanked it free. Unbalanced, Silver fell onto his back, his arms and one leg floundering like he was an ugly cockroach in its death throes.

Thaddeus laughed.

Juniper looked shocked, but in a pleased way.

Silver roared and did his best to roll onto his rotund belly and haul himself upright.

Thaddeus tossed the peg leg over his shoulder. 'Fetch,' he said, then added bravely, 'See how you like it, you mangy mutt!'

'I say, old chap, shhh,' warned Juniper. 'It's like waving a red flag at a bull.'

'A one-legged bull,' said Thaddeus, laughing.

But his laughter died as one of the crew retrieved the peg leg and handed it to Silver. He deftly reattached it to the stump of his knee, then picked up the whip and flicked it lightning-quick at Thaddeus.

Thaddeus danced across the deck out of reach of the hateful weapon. 'You haven't got your Captain yet, which means you can't harm a hair on my head, remember?'

Silver was furious. He took his rage out on

the pail instead of Thaddeus, knocking it flying with his peg leg and showering Juniper with dirty suds. Juniper spluttered, but said nothing, staring with wide-eyed admiration at Thaddeus.

The look seemed to fan Silver's fury. He took off after Thaddeus.

'I'LL NOT BE HARMIN' NO HAIR ON YER HEAD!' he roared. 'I'LL BE HARMIN' THE HEAD BENEATH THE HAIR!'

Thaddeus hadn't expected that! And an angry pirate with a peg leg and a whip wasn't something to negotiate with. He ran, sprinting along the deck, around the mizzenmast, and made for the hatch that Skip had disappeared into earlier.

This seemed to enrage Silver further.

'GRAB 'IM, YE SCURVY DOGS, BEFORE HE ESCAPES BELOW!'

A hand stretched forth and Thaddeus was lifted up off the deck with his feet still running through empty air.

'In the sea chest – now!' ordered Silver.

The pirate dropped Thaddeus into the chest and he tumbled down the steps. Juniper was thrown in after him.

'Oomph!' Thaddeus said when Juniper landed on top of him.

'I say, awfully sorry, old chap.'

Thaddeus rolled out from beneath his friend feeling considerably flattened.

'Let that be a lesson to ye,' said Silver, blocking the sunlight with his bushy head. 'I bain't be havin' no mutiny on me own ship, and ye be doin' well to heed me rules, includin' never goin' below decks.'

He slammed the lid shut, and Thaddeus heard the thudding of running feet as Silver shouted, 'WHAT BE YE LOOKIN' AT, YE FILTHY DOGS? BACK TO WORK!'

Thaddeus bounded up the steps and shoved at the lid with his shoulder. It was fastened firm and he slapped it in frustration. He was rewarded with a spiteful clomp from above.

'It's not even your ship, you stupid thieving pirate!' Thaddeus yelled. 'Just you wait till I tell Pepperjack what you said!'

He slumped miserably on the bottom step and looked at Juniper's unhappy face. 'Aww, I'm sorry, Jupe, but did you see him bash Skip?'

Juniper nodded. 'If you're going to look for the third child in Safe Harbour, we need to know more about the place. I think I read about it in one of the books over there.'

'Which one?' asked Thaddeus, looking at the bookshelves that lined one wall.

'Can't remember, but I do remember it said

that Safe Harbour is the safest place in the Seven Seas for anyone in trouble. It has some sort of magic surrounding it. You'll be safe there, old chap, the pirates won't be able to come after you. You might even decide to stay.' His brows knitted in worry.

'What, and leave you here with them?' Thaddeus said, jerking his finger upwards. 'I don't think so.'

'Well, why not, old chap? I've been left before. My parents put me in school and paid the fees, and I've not seen them since. I've had the odd letter or two, and promises to visit in the holidays, but they never turn up. It's almost like they've forgotten I exist. Anyway, you should probably think about it – this could be your only chance to escape and find your mother's dreams.'

'Juniper, I'm coming back! I promise. You'll see!' Juniper's expression remained unchanged so Thaddeus attempted a little light-heartedness. 'You think I'm gonna leave you here to have all the fun by yourself? I don't think so, my friend!'

'But what about your mother's dreams?'

'There'll be another chance to find them. You can help me, after we both get out of here. Deal?'

Thaddeus held out his hand and Juniper promptly shook it.

'It's a deal, old chap. Now all that's left to do is wait for breakfast.'

***

After an hour of waiting, Juniper had begun pacing the sea chest in a highly agitated manner. By lunchtime, he'd given up on breakfast and was pressing his nose against the chest lid trying to lick up the delicious smell of roasting meat that was wafting past on the ocean breeze. It was obvious to Thaddeus that Silver was doing his best to deliberately rub their noses in their punishment.

By dinnertime, the chest lid remained firmly fastened and Juniper had taken to his hammock, clutching his noisy stomach with both hands. His face was drawn and tired. His hands remained on his bulging belly long after he'd fallen asleep.

Thaddeus watched him with sorry eyes. It wasn't fair that Silver had punished Juniper for something Thaddeus had done. He'd never thought he could hate anyone so much, but Silver was certainly proving him wrong.

Thaddeus lay awake all through the long night, plotting his revenge. He considered whittling down Silver's peg leg an inch or two. Or maybe he could simply push him overboard when the *Black*

Wyddah was under full sail. This brought a smile to Thaddeus's lips because it was a permanent solution. By the time anyone realised that Silver was missing, it would be too late.

'Sink …' muttered Juniper, tossing and turning in his sleep.

Thaddeus shuddered as he remembered Silver's threat. If the person who went to Safe Harbour didn't return, the other one would go swimming. No doubt that was causing Juniper's restless dreams.

***

It was several days before Silver's rage was spent, and during that time Thaddeus and Juniper remained locked in the chest. Thaddeus wondered if Skip had been banished to the sail-repair room again. Juniper wore a groove into the floor with all his pacing. The only time he ceased was when a grubby tattooed arm opened the lid of the chest and handed down their meal trays.

One morning when they were woken by the sound of the lid opening, it was Skip's head that poked through. Thaddeus noticed the big lump on his arm with yellow bruising where Silver had whacked Skip with his peg leg and fresh hatred for the pirate streaked through him.

'Can we come out yet?' asked Juniper. He was looking at the dust motes that danced tauntingly in the rays of sun that bounced off the steps.

Skip pointed at Thaddeus. 'Silver says ye be coming with me.'

Juniper moved forwards hopefully, but Skip put a hand up to stop him. 'Ye be staying and eating yer breakfast.' He shoved a laden tray towards Juniper, and watched guardedly as Thaddeus climbed the steps.

The brightness outside was dazzling after the dimness of the chest and it took Thaddeus's eyes a moment to adjust. When they did, he was surprised to see that they were no longer surrounded entirely by ocean. In the distance he could make out a hazy line of land that curved into a harbour full of tall-masted ships and smaller fishing vessels.

'That be Safe Harbour,' Skip said as he led Thaddeus towards the quarterdeck, where Silver was peering through a spyglass. 'That be where ye be going to get the last child.'

'Did I tell ye to speak?' growled Silver, lowering the spyglass and clipping Skip around the ear.

Skip stood mutely to one side.

'That be far enough,' Silver said, making sure Thaddeus was a safe distance from his peg leg. 'Ye best be listenin' and rememberin', boy, 'cause I only be sayin' this once. We be settin' anchor in no time, and ye be gettin' in one of those little boats so Skip can row ye to Safe Harbour.'

Thaddeus looked at Skip's scrawny arms. He doubted that Skip could row anywhere and fear formed a knot in his stomach.

'Ye listenin', boy?' Thaddeus nodded, but Silver hobbled closer and gave his ear a nasty flick anyway before continuing. 'When yer feet touch dry land, ye be havin' till sunset to get the child and bring it back –'

'Wait – how will I know where to find the right child?' Thaddeus asked. 'And how can I make them come willingly? It's not as if I can chuck them in a sack and sling them over my shoulder, is it?'

His tone was laden with sarcasm, which clearly didn't improve Silver's mood.

'Ye be havin' a smart mouth and no doubt a smart head too,' snarled the pirate. 'Ye'll be workin' it out – if ye know what's good for yer fat friend.' He pointed at the sea chest. 'He bain't goin' to float for long in a deep salty bath.'

'You can't do that. You'll never find your

Captain then,' said Thaddeus.

Silver grinned and Thaddeus experienced a tingle of discomfort. 'Ye better not be thinkin' of crossin' me, boy. For I be tellin' ye this – if ye fail me, don't ever be leavin' Safe Harbour or I'll be catchin' up with ye.' He stroked the pistol stuck through the scarlet sash around his thick waist, his meaning very clear.

'In that case I'll need to take Booth or Henry with me,' said Thaddeus. 'They can carry the child when I find him or her.'

Silver laughed like a maniac. 'I needs Booth and I be wantin' Henry,' he mimicked in a whiny tone.

Thaddeus felt a blanket of rage swathe his body. He clenched his hands. His eyes fell on the pirate's peg leg and he wondered whether Silver had a spare on board. He was very tempted to yank it again, but this time he would toss it into the frothy white waves that hugged the sides of the *Wyddah*.

Silver read his thoughts and pushed his face close to Thaddeus's. His eyes were bloodshot and his breath was vile. Thaddeus swore he saw a wad of ham caught between the pirate's yellowed teeth.

'Don't even be thinkin' on it,' Silver rasped,

'or ye'll be flyin' after it to fetch it.'

'Let me take Booth at least,' persisted Thaddeus.

'He can't,' Skip said. 'None of us be able to set foot on Safe Harbour or we be shrivelling up and dying. There be a safety spell on it. No pirates, nobody who intends harm to another, has ever been coming back from there. All we be knowing is that they come to a sticky end.'

Skip's revelation earned him another cuff from Silver.

Thaddeus filed the information away and looked at the horizon. The ship was so close to land now that he could see the leaves on the trees. They were flickering in the warm island breeze and looked like tinsel. The thought reminded him of the happy Christmases he'd spent with his family, and he pushed the memory away.

'Ready the anchor!' roared Silver. 'Lower the flag and trim the sails, ye lazy dogs, before I be trimmin' yer ears.'

Thaddeus watched the bustle that was required to bring the *Black Wyddah* to a stop. The ship's sails drooped like wet rags, and pirates the size of ants scurried along the topmost rigging to roll and tie them. The anchor was dropped and Thaddeus listened to its groan as it sank to the seabed.

He felt torn. Safe Harbour sounded nice, and it certainly looked nice. Even more important, it was a refuge from the treacherous sea. He could stay there until he worked out where to find his mother's dreams and how to get back home. Hope glimmered in his mind. But then it was replaced by an image of Juniper and the promise Thaddeus had made to him.

Thaddeus sighed and let go of the glimmer of hope. He couldn't leave Juniper. He couldn't break his promise to his friend. Safe Harbour would still be there another time – for them both.

He was so lost in thought that he almost jumped out of his skin when Skip tapped him on the shoulder and pointed him towards the rowboat that was waiting to be lowered to the sea. Thaddeus got in with a sinking feeling. It was decided. He would find the third child and bring him or her back to the *Wyddah* and her crew.

CHAPTER SIX

SAFE HARBOUR

Skip surprised Thaddeus with his rowing ability. It took him next to no time to row past the larger vessels resting at anchor, weave between the barrels bobbing on the surface that marked lowered crab pots, and finally overtake another longboat bulging and groaning under the weight of a tired crew.

'This be as far as I goes,' said Skip, folding the oars and letting the boat nudge against the dock between a loaded ship and a smelly fishing vessel.

'So you'll wait for me?' asked Thaddeus.

Skip nodded, but Thaddeus didn't move.

'How will I know which child is the right one?' he asked despairingly. 'It's not the same for me as it was for the pirates – I don't have Noxious's magic to guide me.'

Skip sat thoughtfully for a moment, then said,

'Ye be having something better than magic. Ye be having that compass inside you, right here.' He placed his hand over his heart. 'I feel it growing in me too. Ye just need to believe it be showing ye true north and follow its direction. Ye best be going now. Silver only be giving ye till sunset.'

Thaddeus clambered out of the rowboat, which was no easy feat as the water level was quite a lot lower than the top of the dock. He watched Skip row away, presumably to wait out of sight until he returned.

Feeling not at all hopeful, Thaddeus turned and dragged his feet along the barrel-laden dock. He passed gangways filled with wicker baskets of freshly caught fish, and wooden cages holding cooing pigeons, and even a braying donkey. It looked like it was market day at Safe Harbour.

Nobody paid him any mind. No one sought him out to ask what his business was there. In fact, he might have been invisible. He supposed the people milling around on the dock assumed that he wasn't about to do them any harm or he wouldn't have been able to step onto land. He picked up his pace, aware of Silver's eyes penetrating the small of his back through his spyglass.

The dock was T-shaped, and as he turned

into the main section it became more crowded. He had to dodge the sweaty backs of men hauling their cargo to shore. He followed an ant-like line of people to the end of the dock, and crossed a pebbly beach before reaching a mountain of steps that wound their way up to the village. He passed a smokehouse that was drying yesterday's catch. It wasn't the most pleasant of smells, but it reminded him that he hadn't eaten breakfast.

A group of ragged children came squealing up from the beach. They dodged between the burdened adults and raced past Thaddeus up the steps. He eyed them eagerly and followed them, ignoring the burning of his leg muscles, but they disappeared into the throng of people at the top.

Thaddeus had never been anywhere like Safe Harbour. It looked like a scene on a holiday picture postcard. The streets were cobbled, and the whitewashed buildings gleamed in the sunlight. There were old men mending nets, and young women sweeping doorsteps. They all smiled nicely at him when he passed. The smell from a bakery made his stomach beg for food, but he went on, following the shouts of vendors to a crowded market in the town square.

A clutch of chickens had broken free of their cage, and their harried owner, squawking more loudly than the chickens themselves, was darting through the crowd trying to scoop up his escapees. Thaddeus swooped down to lend him a hand, and when all the chickens were recaptured the grateful owner handed him a silver coin.

He considered making his way back to the bakery, but the crowd was thick and he was conscious of time ticking away, so he moved towards a fruit stall, where he handed his easily gained silver to a withered hand. In return, he was given the ripest, juiciest apple he'd ever laid eyes on. He sank his teeth into it right away and for a moment he felt like everything was right in the world.

The feeling lasted until he'd finished the apple, and then the burden of responsibility and the discomforting image of Juniper floundering in the ocean sank into the pit of his stomach. He shoved what was left of the apple core through the bars of a nearby cage, where a plump pig snuffled and snorted over it.

He found a spot a short distance from the market square, sat down, closed his eyes and concentrated on finding the compass inside his heart. But it didn't seem to be working. There was too much going on inside him. Too many directions. He missed his parents – but thinking of them hurt his heart. He wanted to go home, but there was the problem of his mother's stolen dreams. He'd made a promise to find them and bring them back to her. And he would, but he'd made a promise to Juniper too – that he would return to the *Wyddah* so they could escape together. He couldn't keep both promises at the same time. Which way was his true north?

He sat there pondering the problem until the sun had passed high overhead and was beginning to lower itself on the other side of the horizon. He still had no idea what to do. In fact, the lower the sun sank, the further away direction seemed to be.

From his vantage point Thaddeus could see the fishing vessels coming home and the fishermen unloading their catch. The market had emptied and the stall holders were packing up their wares. The wind picked up, bringing with it a fine mist.

Silver had given him until sunset to find the last child, which meant he only had a couple of hours left. He couldn't sit here and wait for direction, or for the last child to fall into his lap. He needed to do something!

A group of sailors passed by and he heard one of them say, 'We'll sort it out at *The Imp's Cup*

– you still owe me a nip.'

The word 'imp' brought Thaddeus to his feet, the third child forgotten.

He followed the men up the hill to a stone building with moss creeping up its sides. Squatting out the front were several wooden tables and shining iron chairs. The sailors entered the tavern and Thaddeus was left outside. The barkeeper came out and began clearing the tables and clinking glasses. Thaddeus smiled, but the man didn't smile back, just stared.

Thaddeus hurried past, thinking that *The Imp's Cup* didn't seem a very friendly place, unlike the rest of Safe Harbour. Which meant it might be just the type of place that was a haven for a thieving shadow-imp!

The distant ringing of a bell echoed across the land and out to sea. The mist crept closer. Thaddeus moved off the path and ducked behind the building. He wanted to peek inside *The Imp's Cup* to see if he could glimpse his mother's dreams or the shadow-imp. He told himself he wasn't choosing the dreams over Juniper – he was just looking.

He was sneaking up to a back window when the door opened. Thaddeus shot into the bushes and watched while a burly man brought out a bag of rubbish. He marched straight towards the bush where Thaddeus was hiding. Thaddeus shrank further back and wriggled between two large trees whose branches hugged overhead to form an arch. He rested his back against the trunk of one tree … and immediately wished he hadn't. Something was sticking his back to the wood. He moved his arm up to try and unstick himself but that only made matters worse. His hand was now stuck too, in an awkward V-shape above his head.

'Arrgh!'

He tried to move his head to the side to see what had him fastened so tightly, but it was stuck too. He pulled all his weight forwards and was rewarded with brief movement before he sprang back like a rubber band. His whole body reverberated and his eyes blurred.

When the shuddering stopped, he noticed a bit of what looked like fine net hanging down the trunk beside him. It must have dislodged when he moved. *Funny place to hang a net*, he thought, straining his eyes sideways and trying to stretch forwards again.

He was on his third attempt, with beads of sweat trickling down his hot face, when he heard a girl whisper, 'I wouldn't do that if I were you.'

Thaddeus swivelled his eyeballs and saw

a scruffy girl standing stiffly at the edge of his limited vision. Her face was smudged with dirt, and a twig hung from the strands of her ratty brown hair. She was wearing a sack-like tunic with two pockets that was as filthy as her face and Thaddeus thought she needed a good hosing down. She looked about eleven, the same age as him.

'Well, I'm not exactly doing it for fun,' he said, feeling more than irritated, 'I'm actually stuck.'

'I know,' said the girl and she looked uneasily up at the overarching branches. 'You must be stupid, you know, to lean against a web the size of a large boat.'

Thaddeus couldn't believe her nerve. 'Listen here, no one invited you along so why don't you just clear –' Something suddenly registered in his mind. 'W-what did you say?'

'I'd keep still. Spiders are alerted to food by the wobbling of their web. And you're wobbling enough to signal a small buffet. Although by the look of you, I'd say the spider's going to be sorely disappointed. You're all bone.'

Thaddeus froze so completely that the only part of him still moving was his pounding heart and the great drops of sweat sliding down his face.

'Did you say a web?' he whispered, barely moving his lips.

The girl nodded and Thaddeus felt panic seize him. This was way worse than being kidnapped by pirates.

'Help!' he spluttered.

The girl flicked her ratty hair over her shoulder. 'Help – what?'

'Are you kidding me? Help, *please*,' hissed Thaddeus.

'That's better.'

The girl crept forwards silently on bare feet, then dug a hand in the pocket of her tunic, her eyes never leaving the overhead branches. Thaddeus thought she looked more alert than a meerkat at the zoo. Her hand came out of her tunic empty but curled into a fist, as if she held something. But Thaddeus couldn't see anything. She quickly moved to the web and moved her hand in a nicking motion around the stickiness that had trapped Thaddeus's feet, her eyes still searching the branches above.

'Are you a complete head case?' he said between clenched teeth. 'You need a stick or … or a stone – something sharp. A knife would be preferable, but seeing as we –'

The girl stopped what she was doing and stood

so her nose was almost touching Thaddeus's. Her green eyes had become cloudy, like the colour of the sea on a stormy day.

'For your information, boy-who-is-stupid-enough-to-get-stuck-in-a-spider's-web, I *do* have a knife. You just can't see it – no one can. And it's not just a normal knife, it's sharper. So if you don't mind …'

She bent and resumed nicking the web and, to Thaddeus's surprise, he felt his feet come free. The girl stood and sliced around his head, like he was a cut-out doll in a picture book. He heard a scrape as the knife came close to his ears and he flinched.

'Keep still,' she hissed.

'You think I'm not gonna move when you're cutting so close to my face?' he whispered back, fear increasing his irritation. 'You're not even watching! What are you looking for anyway – is the spider coming?'

The girl paused again and glowered at him. 'First of all, I'm actually doing you a favour. Second of all, I'm not the head case who left the path to lean against a monstrous spider's web –'

'Well, actually you did leave the path, so you can talk.'

The girl made a great show of dropping her

invisible knife back into her pocket and took a deliberate step away from Thaddeus, whose left side was still firmly stuck to the web.

'Third of all,' she said, smirking as she folded her arms across her chest, 'I happen to be looking up because that's where the spider will be. But I guess you already knew that, didn't you?'

Thaddeus felt his stomach descend dangerously close to his underpants.

'What are you doing – why are you stopping?' he squeaked. 'I'm still stuck … quick … knife … don't … just … stand … there!' Terror garbled his words together.

The girl stood silently with her arms still folded.

'I'm sorry … please … please, just hurry – it could pounce any second,' he ground out through his teeth.

His apology calmed the girl's stormy eyes and she delved back into her pocket, brought out her invisible knife and began slicing around him again.

'What's your name anyway?' he asked in an effort to distract himself from how long it was taking her.

'Molly Mallou,' she answered. 'Yours?'

'Thaddeus Bix. Can't you speed up? It's nearly dinnertime!'

Thaddeus had given up trying to keep still. He frantically tugged at his still stuck limbs with web-wobbling force. The girl ignored the comment and his tone and helped him pull his leg free. Thaddeus practically fell on top of her in his exultation at finally escaping.

'Now let's get out of here – quietly,' she said.

Thaddeus didn't argue. One look at the mess they'd made of the web and he knew the spider wouldn't be pleased. He intended on being far away by the time it found out.

He took a step forwards and his foot landed on a dry twig and snapped it in half. The crack was very loud in the silent air.

The girl glared at him. Thaddeus glared back, until he saw her eyes bulge like a goldfish's. He suddenly felt the hairs on the back of his neck prickle. Slowly he turned back to face the web, only it was no longer visible, for dangling in front of it, on a strand as thick as a rope, was an enormous spider.

It had spindly legs as long as flagpoles, and a body the size of a small car. Even more horrifying, its head looked like it belonged to an ogre's grandmother. Its face was peppered with age spots and its skin was wrinkled like a piece of screwed-up paper. Tufts of wispy hair sprouted from the top of its head like the bristles of an old scrubbing brush.

It might be friendly, thought Thaddeus hopefully – a thought which disappeared when the spider opened its cavernous mouth to reveal two fangs the size of elephant tusks and dripping with venom.

CHAPTER SEVEN

THE EYE THAT SEES

Thaddeus gulped and stepped backwards, placing himself slightly behind Molly. It made sense – after all, she was the one holding the knife that had wrecked the spider's web. He totally forgot that the knife was invisible.

Molly gave him a filthy look but held her ground, her hand still clenched around her knife. Thaddeus couldn't deny that he felt relieved. Who wouldn't with a ginormous spider gnashing its venomous fangs inches from your skin?

The spider dropped itself lower and folded its spindly legs beneath it. The action brought its head almost level with Molly and Thaddeus, who was seriously starting to wonder why he didn't just run. Molly had made it quite clear that she didn't need saving, so why should he hang around? It wasn't as if he didn't have other things that needed dealing with.

He began to back away. The spider shot out a strand of web and Thaddeus stilled instantly. There was no way he was getting tangled in that again. He moved back alongside Molly.

The spider leaned towards them and Thaddeus saw its sightless eye sockets. It licked its wizened lips and breathed in deeply.

'Sisters,' it hissed excitedly, clicking its fangs together, 'it smells good. Bring me the eye.'

'Sisters!!!' Thaddeus groaned. Of all the bad luck.

Two more spiders, as old and ugly as the first, lowered themselves from the tree branches. The smallest pulled something milky from beneath the folds of an eye socket and handed it to the first spider, which grabbed it greedily and pushed it hurriedly into its own empty socket.

'Sisters! The eye sees all,' it said triumphantly. 'The boy would do harm. The girl too, but the boy is the dangerous one – he has awoken the darkness. We must cut the thread of his life now. Snip it before it is too late. Then we shall suck their juices.'

Thaddeus couldn't tell what Molly was feeling because she remained silently expressionless. But the spider's words had ignited a fuse of fear within him. If he didn't get away soon, there was sure to be a nasty explosion that would leave much more than a skiddy in his underpants! He crossed his trembling legs while his eyes hunted for a way out. All he could think of were Skip's words about people coming to a sticky end. He wondered if he was in this mess because he'd thought about leaving Juniper. But he wouldn't have, so it wasn't fair that the spiders were saying he was someone who would do harm to others.

He opened his mouth to tell them this, but his tongue was sticky with fright and no sound came out.

'You are mistaken,' Molly told the spider, finally finding her voice. 'I mean no harm.'

'Let me see, sister, let me see.'

The second spider raised a leg and waved it towards the spider with the eye. The flailing leg knocked the eye out of the first spider's socket, and it landed on the ground and rolled towards Thaddeus's foot. It was the size of a soccer ball.

The spiders scrambled around in a panic, searching for it.

'Where is it?' snapped the first spider.

'We are sightless without it,' moaned the smallest one.

'Shut up and find it,' ordered the first.

Thaddeus grinned and uncrossed his legs. Triumph flooded through him, washing away the fear. *Must be my lucky day*, he thought, picking up the eye. He screwed up his face as his hands came into contact with the snot-like mucus that coated it.

'I have the eye,' he said, his tone as soft as a cat toying with a mouse.

The scrambling spiders came to an abrupt halt.

'Now look what you've done!' the first spider scolded its sisters.

The other two hunched themselves into meek bows, their faces masks of worry. 'We're sorry, sister,' they grovelled.

Thaddeus knew that he held a very powerful bargaining chip, even though he hated the feeling of the snot stuff dripping down his arm like dog drool. Not to mention the unnerving fact that the eye was swivelling back and forth as if trying to see something.

'I'll give it back if you promise not to harm me or Molly,' said Thaddeus.

'You do not know what a promise means,' spat the first spider. It tried to swat at Thaddeus with a leg and missed by a mile.

Thaddeus snickered. 'You're as blind as a

stupid bat in daylight.'

Molly stomped hard on his foot. 'What are you doing?' she hissed.

'Ahem, I mean, last chance,' he told the spider.

It swung again, closer this time, and hissed with fury when its leg sliced through empty air.

Thaddeus couldn't help himself. 'You stupid insect! Molly, where's your knife? You know, the one that could make mincemeat out of a giant eye!'

The spiders quickly huddled together, obviously debating how to deal with this new threat. It took them only a minute to reach a decision, much to Thaddeus's relief. His whole arm was feeling uncomfortably moist from the eye's snotty covering.

'If you give us back our eye, we shall count to five before we come after you,' said the first spider. 'Are we agreed?'

'We don't think so,' said Molly, shaking her head.

'No, we don't,' chimed in Thaddeus.

'Take it or leave it,' snapped the spider. 'But I warn you, the eye will soon feel heavy in your hands for it carries the weight of all that has been seen, all that is seen and all that will be seen. You will soon grow tired and then we shall get it back anyway, and you tasty morsels along with it.'

'You don't seem to be listening,' Molly said. 'You won't have an eye left after –'

But Thaddeus cut her off. 'It's right – the eye's already making my arm ache,' he whispered. Then something occurred to him. 'What do you mean about the eye carrying the weight of all it has seen?' he asked loudly.

The question was to the largest of the spider sisters, but it was the smallest one that answered.

'Just like a human – stupid in the face of death. It's what it means, *stupid*!' It emphasised the word, causing two red spots to leap onto Thaddeus's cheeks. 'The eye sees all. It can show you anything you ask it to. Anything from the past, the present or the fut–'

'Hey! Who are you calling stupid?' Molly yelled. 'We're the ones holding the eye *and a kni*–'

'Hush!' spat the older spider, silencing its sisters and Molly.

But it was too late. Thaddeus understood the power he was holding in his hands and the realisation sent a warm glow cascading through him.

'Ohhh,' he said. 'So if I were to say, for example, oh, eye, please show me where my mother's dreams are …'

The eye immediately grew murky.

'Enough!' spat the older spider. It stepped forward and clicked its fangs. 'The eye is not yours to command.'

Molly lunged, her arm outstretched, and sliced her knife across the spider's leg. The spider howled and stumbled backwards. Its two sisters collapsed in fright at the sound of its pain.

'What is it?' they cried. 'What happened?'

'Don't you dare come any closer!' Molly yelled. She grabbed hold of Thaddeus's arm and tried to drag him away, but he shook her off. 'Come on! What are you doing?' she hissed.

'Look … it's showing me what I asked for!'

The murkiness of the eye was forming into an image, and Thaddeus found himself staring at the shadow-imp, as clearly as if he were looking at it through a bus window. The imp was crouched on a man's chest, playing his panpipe and stealing the man's dreams in the same way it had stolen Thaddeus's mother's dreams. The silvery net appeared, and as soon as the poor fellow's dreams were in its hands the imp jubilantly skipped away. The eye followed it as it moved through the shadows, disappearing into one and emerging from another some distance away.

'What is that and where is it going?' asked

Molly as she watched the eye with almost the same amount of interest as Thaddeus.

'It's a shadow-imp,' explained Thaddeus, 'and it stole my mother's dreams. Quickly – show me,' he ordered the eye. 'Where are my mother's dreams?'

The eye spun and what they were seeing moved forwards like a speeding car. Landscapes blurred by and then slowed at a building. The walls dissolved, showing rows and rows of shelves loaded with small jars, the glowing dreams flickering within.

'Yes!' said Thaddeus exultantly, gripping the eye tight. 'But where is it? Where's the building?'

The eye zoomed its focus outwards and Thaddeus saw the outside of a dark warehouse with a sign that read *Grimbles*. Then the eye zoomed further out, showing a map. Thaddeus glimpsed the flash of writing before the eye blinked and the sight faded.

'Anatolia,' he said to Molly. 'Do you know where that is?'

'Across the ocean,' she said. 'Now let me have a turn.'

She reached for the eye but Thaddeus turned away from her. 'So I'd need a boat,' he said, thinking out loud.

'Yes. Now give me the eye – I want to ask it something,' snapped Molly, reaching for it once more.

But Thaddeus wasn't done yet. He looked towards the spiders. He'd been so engrossed in what the eye was showing him that he hadn't realised how quiet they'd become, nor how the light had dimmed. The sun was setting and he knew Silver wouldn't wait beyond the last ray disappearing beneath the horizon. Thaddeus needed to get back to the *Wyddah* and he could only do that if he found what the pirates wanted.

'Show me the last child,' he commanded the eye.

'Hey, it's my turn!' Molly said. 'You've had your –'

Thaddeus cut her off. 'You watch the spiders, then you can have your turn.'

The eye was becoming murky again and then suddenly it cleared.

'Thaddeus ... um, we might want to think about leaving ...' Molly's voice had become tight.

Thaddeus tore his gaze away from the eye just in time to see the spiders separating into a semicircle. They scuttled forwards, intending to surround him and Molly.

'Thaddeus!' Molly cried.

She backed into him, almost knocking the eye out of his hands. He looked down and couldn't believe what the eye was showing him.

'Time is up, small human,' hissed the oldest spider. 'Give us the eye.'

'I have an idea,' Thaddeus whispered to Molly. 'Get ready to run and follow me.'

'We're waiting,' said the spider.

'You want the eye?' Thaddeus asked. 'Well, you can have it!'

And he booted it like a football, right into the oldest spider's legs. It rebounded off them and rolled between the legs of the other two.

'GET IT!' screamed the first spider, knocking its sisters onto their backs as it scrambled towards the milky orb.

'Run!' hissed Thaddeus, tearing back towards the path.

'You shouldn't have done that. They'll be after us as soon as they find their eye,' Molly shouted, sprinting down the hill alongside him.

'This is Safe-flipping-Harbour! What are they doing having people-eating spiders here? Follow me – I know a place where they won't be able to get us.'

They disappeared into the damp mist, Thaddeus darting this way and that as he led them away from the spiders. They leapt over a stile, raced back through the village that now twinkled with lights, past the market square, and down the steps to the pebbled beach where empty boats, crab pots and a tangle of fishing nets lay.

It wasn't long before they heard hissing and loud scuttling sounds behind them.

'This way,' puffed Thaddeus, leaping onto the deserted dock. The snapping of angry fangs was getting closer.

'SKIP!' yelled Thaddeus.

Skip manoeuvred the small boat just in time to catch Thaddeus as he launched himself off the end of the dock. He landed with a thud and spun around to see Molly hesitating, clearly not wanting to go near the water.

'Jump!' he screamed. 'They're right behind you!'

A webbed net soared through the mist and landed on the edge of the dock. But Molly had already jumped. She landed in the boat right on top of Thaddeus.

'ROW!' he shouted.

Skip didn't need to be told twice. Three humungous hairy shapes were taking form through the mist and the sound of twenty-four spindly legs clipping on the wooden planks and six angrily clicking fangs was enough to set his arms going like a windmill on a blustery day.

Thaddeus let out a breath of relief as the boat sped away and the spiders' fury at losing their prey faded to a distant squabble.

'Phew, that was close,' he said.

'You think?' said Molly sarcastically, rolling up her sleeves and fanning her flushed and sweaty face.

Thaddeus ignored her tone, for his heart was singing. It was indeed his lucky day. The eye had shown him all he had needed to know, and Molly Mallou had quite literally landed in his lap.

CHAPTER EIGHT

BELOW THE HATCH

Molly looked more frightened in the boat than she had standing in front of the spiders. She frowned murderously at Skip every time he lifted the oars and sent splashes her way. Thaddeus gathered that, like him, Molly didn't like water. But given the choice between being in a boat on the water and facing three angry spiders, Thaddeus knew which he would choose.

'You can stop rowing now,' said Molly stiffly to Skip. 'We'll just sit here and wait till they go back to their trees.' She cocked her head to the side. 'Shouldn't take too long. I think I can hear them clicking back along the dock.'

Skip continued his windmill movements, propelling them further out to sea.

'Oi! I said you can stop rowing now!' yelled Molly.

'We're not going back,' said Thaddeus quietly. 'He's taking us to the ship.'

A frown darkened Molly's face. 'I don't want to go to no ship. Take me back to Safe Harbour this instant – I insist! There's a little cove just along from the dock – you can let me off there.'

Skip kept his head down and his arms moving. The creaking of the *Black Wyddah* floated towards them over the mist-blanketed sea. It wouldn't be long before the rowboat bumped alongside her hull – and just in time, Thaddeus thought, for the sun was sinking below the horizon.

'I say!' cried Molly, sounding a lot like Juniper. She stood up, causing one side of the boat to tip perilously close to the frothing sea. 'Turn around immediately!'

'Sit down, would you!' said Thaddeus, clutching the edge of the boat. 'I can't swim.'

The words shocked Molly into sitting. Obviously she couldn't swim either.

'We can't go back,' Thaddeus told her.

'The spiders will have given up and gone by now,' she said.

'It's not because of the spiders. It's because of who we are.'

Molly was speechless with anger.

The eerie lanterns and ghostly shape of the

Black Wyddah oozed out of the mist. The rowboat scraped against wood and Skip called up to the pirates hidden above. Four ropes were thrown down. Skip tied them onto the rowboat and, with plenty of loud grunts, the small boat was lifted quickly from the sea and up onto the *Wyddah*'s deck. Rough, blistered hands reached for them and hauled them out like a prized catch.

Molly, looking a lot more secure now that she was on solid footing, was the first to speak. 'I demand to be taken back at once. Who's in charge here? I want to see him.' She stamped her bare foot angrily.

Silver thrust through the throng of pirates with Noxious alongside him.

'You managed it,' said Noxious, as if he hadn't believed that Thaddeus would succeed.

Silver grabbed Molly's arm and pulled her close. 'Ye be wantin' to see who be in charge? Ye be lookin' at 'im,' he snarled.

'You're not the Captain,' sneered Molly. 'I insist you take me to your Captain!'

'Ye'll be seeing the Captain alright,' said Silver with a grin. He turned to the crew and roared, 'Chuck 'em in the chest! Look lively, me hearties, and heave away. They be takin' us to Pepperjack very soon.'

He clomped away, the sound punctuated by his mad laughter. As Noxious followed, Thaddeus heard Silver say to the wizard, 'It be time! Now ye be tellin' us how we be usin' the brats' compass to find the Captain.'

Two pirates picked up Thaddeus and Molly, tossed them over their shoulders and carried them to the sea chest. Thaddeus looked back and met Skip's eyes. The expression on Skip's face was one of utmost terror.

Thaddeus's heart gave a painful jerk. He knew without a doubt that facing Captain Pepperjack would be worse than facing the three spider sisters and their poisonous fangs.

***

Thaddeus and Molly tumbled down the steps into the sea chest, and Juniper let out a sound like a balloon when all the air rushes out of it.

'I say, that took forever,' he told Thaddeus. 'I thought you might not be coming back! How did you find her?'

As he spoke, he bent to help Molly to her feet, but she slapped his hand away.

'Steady on!' said Juniper.

'Don't speak to me and don't touch me,' she

said, and swung herself into the nearest hammock.

Juniper shrugged and looked askance at Thaddeus.

'She found me,' said Thaddeus, answering Juniper's earlier question. 'She followed me all the way into the boat.'

Juniper scratched his head in puzzlement. He looked from Thaddeus to Molly and back to Thaddeus again, before clearing his throat awkwardly. 'I say, old chap ... she *followed* you? What are you – the Pied Piper? I mean, at the risk of sounding rude, you're not exactly followable. In fact, you look downright unfollowable. Really, I mean no offence,' he added hurriedly, noting Thaddeus's frown. 'I mean, it's not just you – she doesn't exactly look like the kind of person that would follow ... I say, what's that stuff stuck to the back of your head?' Juniper reached out and a strand of spider's web the width of his thumb stuck to his hand. He held it close to his face, his eyes taking on an animated glow. 'Is it ... I say, did you go to a fair and have fairy floss? I love fairy floss. Did you save me –'

'It isn't fairy floss, you fatty,' Molly snapped.

Juniper looked wounded. He mumbled something incoherent before lumbering over to his hammock and climbing inside.

'Don't you call him that!' said Thaddeus furiously. 'Just because you're in a foul mood doesn't mean you have to share it around. You've only got yourself to blame. No one asked you to come and rescue me.'

'Rescue?' Juniper's mouth formed a perfect circle.

'And no one made you jump into the boat, nor tied you to it once you were in it,' Thaddeus went on. 'Besides, it's not as if Juniper and I want to be here either!'

Molly rose from her hammock in one angry bound. 'You ungrateful little wretch! I should have left you to those giant spiders – you'd certainly look better in pieces!'

'Giant spiders?' squeaked Juniper.

'And for your information, if you hadn't led me to that dead-end dock I wouldn't have needed to jump into your stupid boat. And ... and ...' Molly floundered to a stop.

Thaddeus eyed her suspiciously. What was she keeping back?

'You got something more you want to say?' he asked.

Molly turned slightly pink and turned her back on Thaddeus, but she didn't return to her hammock. Instead she began pacing up and down the sea chest like a ferocious caged tiger.

'Giant spiders?' Juniper said again, his eyes bulging.

Thaddeus filled him in on the last few hours.

'And they call it Safe Harbour?' asked Juniper, tucking his legs up into his hammock while his eyes scanned the shadows around them. 'Doesn't sound that safe to me.'

'That's what I said,' agreed Thaddeus.

Molly spun around. 'At least it was safer than being stuck on a ship full of pirates!'

She looked disheartened and Thaddeus felt a little bit sorry for her. 'Look, I am sorry, Molly, but I didn't really have a choice. It wasn't my fault.'

'Oh, you had a choice alright,' she said, and glared at them both with murderous intent.

Thaddeus lost his temper. He'd said he was sorry. What more did she want? 'You think I had a choice? You have no idea what I've been through!'

'You!' she snapped. 'This isn't about you!'

'I say, you both need to calm down. You'll bring the –'

Juniper didn't finish what he was saying because Molly's fist shot out and biffed him squarely on the jaw. He fell out of the hammock, stunned.

Thaddeus, whose temper was equal to Molly's,

dived on top of her and pulled her away from Juniper. This only intensified her anger and she let rip into Thaddeus with both hands, scratching his face and pulling his hair.

'You lying, thieving sneak!' she screamed.

Thaddeus completely forgot everything he'd ever been taught about never hitting a girl. A red mist seemed to cover his eyes and the rage that he'd been holding tight inside, ever since he saw his father with the suitcase, came billowing out. He grabbed hold of Molly's hair and pulled it hard, yelling in her face for every single thing that had happened to him since he'd been shoved inside that stinking sack.

'I say, that's no way to treat a girl!' said Juniper, trying to tug Thaddeus away from Molly.

Thaddeus elbowed him in the ribs, but at the same moment Molly got out of Thaddeus's grip. Her teeth bared, she reached into her pocket. Thaddeus knew she had her knife in her hand.

'Watch out, Juniper!' he cried. 'She's got a knife!'

Juniper let out a howl as Molly stalked towards him. The commotion brought the pirates scurrying down the steps into the sea chest.

'She's got a knife,' blubbered Juniper to Booth, who was first down the steps.

Booth took one look at Molly's seemingly empty hands and laughed. 'Ye be goin' mad, tubby. There ain't no knife.'

Molly lashed out at him and the tip of her blade drew a red line across Booth's outstretched palm. He howled with shock.

Silver's head poked through the opening. 'What be all this racket?' he growled.

Booth scrambled up the steps backwards. 'She be 'avin' a sword, Silver, an' it be invisible.'

'Invisible, eh? Ye best be takin' it from her then, Booth.'

Silver pushed Booth back into the sea chest with the tip of his peg and yelled for Noxious.

By the time the wizard arrived, Booth had a panting Molly bundled up in his grasp and multiple cuts along his arms and one on his cheek. He hauled Molly onto the deck and Silver slammed the sea chest's lid shut, locking Thaddeus and Juniper in once more.

Thaddeus climbed the steps and pressed his ear against the lid. He couldn't hear much, only snippets of questions about the knife.

'It seems Noxious is rather interested in that knife,' he told Juniper.

The boys sat on the steps and waited for Molly to be thrown back into the sea chest. However, after hours had gone by it became clear that Silver and Noxious were holding her someplace else.

'I wonder what they've done with her?' asked Juniper as he climbed into his hammock for the night.

Thaddeus yawned and climbed into his own hammock. 'I don't know and I don't care. She's not that nice and probably deserves whatever she gets.'

***

The boys were woken the next morning by the rough lurching of their hammocks. Thaddeus managed to stay put in his, but Juniper wasn't so lucky. He found himself sprawled on the floor of the sea chest. Thunder crashed outside and the sea rolled the *Wyddah* from side to side, making it difficult for him to scramble back to his feet. As soon as he managed to pick himself up, another sharp lurch unbalanced him again. Finally, a bigger surge dumped him back into his hammock, where Thaddeus could see from his green face that he was struggling to keep last night's meal in his belly and not all over the floor.

Thaddeus reached out and grabbed an empty water pail as it rolled past. He swung it towards

Juniper, who quickly grabbed it and immediately heaved into it.

'Oh, that's a bit rough,' he said, his pale face resurfacing above the rim of the bucket.

'About as rough as this sea,' said Thaddeus, gripping hold of his hammock as it swayed violently again. He too was feeling decidedly sick but it didn't have anything to do with the rocking ship. A new fear had caught him in a vice-like grip.

'What if we sink?'

'The *Black Wyddah* sink? I don't think there's any worry of that, old chap. She's been around for hundreds of years.'

'That's just my point – she's old!'

Thaddeus's statement brought the green tinge leaping back onto Juniper's face. 'Least I won't have to worry about feeling hungry today,' he said, his voice muffled inside the pail.

After three more wild lurches, Thaddeus thought he might need to share Juniper's bucket. He was just about to ask, when the lid to the sea chest blew open. At first Thaddeus thought it was because of the violent wind, but then Skip's face appeared, followed closely by his thin sodden body.

'Thought ye might be hungry,' he said, producing two soggy squashed rolls and pushing them at Thaddeus. 'Phew, stinks in 'ere.'

He eyed Juniper, who was still clinging to the pail, and gulped. Thaddeus thought Skip looked as if his own stomach might be heaving too.

Thaddeus took the rolls even though he couldn't face eating them right now. This storm was reminding him that soon they would be facing something much more threatening.

'Skip, what's going to happen to us – you know after Pepperjack is found?' he asked.

Skip's shoulders sagged. 'Don't be knowing that,' he said, but Thaddeus could tell he was lying.

Skip made to dart back up the steps, but Thaddeus leapt out of his hammock and got there first. He blocked Skip's way as the *Wyddah* rolled violently on another wave, almost knocking him over.

'Come on, Skip, it's best we know, then we can prepare ourselves.' He didn't have to try hard for a desperate tone.

'Alrights, I'll tell ye, but ye won't be thanking me for it.' Skip sat down on the bottom step and wrapped his arms around the railing, bracing himself against each lurch of the ship. 'He won't be letting ye go,' he said sadly. 'He'll be making ye one of us, or sending ye to the bottom of the ocean.'

'But that's murder – he can't do that,' Juniper said, sticking his head up out of the pail. 'He'll have the police after him. I say, they're probably after him already. My parents would know by now that I'm missing.'

'Murder ain't anything new for Captain Pepperjack,' said Skip. 'When the Captain be free, there ain't no one who can touch him. The whole world be knowing that he disappeared, and most people be thinking he be dead. So when he be coming back, people be thinking that he be risen from the dead and they be fearing him worse than before. And when he do be back, we'll all be feeling his terror – some more than others. The Captain will be knowing those who helped find him and those who didn't.'

Skip's face foretold that terror and Thaddeus pounced on his fear. 'Will you help us escape, Skip?'

The boy recoiled at the suggestion. 'I daren't! I can't! Silver would be killing me!'

'But what if we help you?' offered Thaddeus. 'You could come with us.'

Skip shook his head emphatically. 'I signed me name to the Captain's contract. I can't be leaving, not until the Captain releases me. Besides, it be too late for escape. Noxious be telling Silver that we be ready to find the Captain any moment now.'

'Well, we won't do it, will we?' Thaddeus said, turning to Juniper. 'And Molly won't help either. Where is she anyway?'

'She ain't be having a choice about it,' whispered Skip, looking even more fearful. 'Noxious be watching over her – and she ain't looking too well this morning.'

Thaddeus felt hate surge through him at the mention of the wizard's name. 'What has he done to her?'

Skip didn't answer. Instead he scuttled past Thaddeus up the steps. 'I be off now, but I'll be leaving the door open for some airs. Best ye stay down here though.'

'Skip – wait! What about Molly? Where is she? What have they done to her?'

But Skip had disappeared into the wind and the rain.

Thaddeus angrily threw the food onto the messy floor and watched it mush with the rest of the wet jumble of things rolling about. Then he ran up the steps, determined to make Skip tell him what had happened to Molly, even if he had to drag him back into the sea chest and sit on him.

But Thaddeus dropped that idea the moment he poked his head up through the open lid and saw the grey-drenched world all around. The towering waves were so high that he couldn't tell where the ocean ended and the sky began. He was about to bolt back down the steps and close the lid of the sea chest, blocking out the terror above, when a loose rope snaked by.

'GRAB THE HALYARDS! CHECK THE SCUPPERS!' Booth roared as he skidded past, the rest of his words shredded by the shrieking wind.

Thaddeus watched in fascinated horror. What was stopping the scurrying pirates from being washed off the deck? Then he saw it – a waterlogged rope tied along the length of the ship from bow to stern. Some of the pirates had tied themselves to it so they could safely fulfil their duties. Others –the stupid ones – were merely holding onto the rope with their hands.

An idea formed in Thaddeus's mind. He ducked back down into the sea chest.

'Jupe, the crew are all tied up at the moment,' he smiled at his choice of words, 'keeping us afloat. So now's the perfect time to go find Molly, then we can hide out together until the sea calms, then escape.'

'I don't know, Thaddeus. Silver said to stay down here or else.' Juniper belched loudly, his face still buried in the pail.

'I don't care what that stinking one-legged pirate said. Come on, Jupe. Anyway, what else can Silver do to us? I mean, he's already starving us. I wouldn't have given those soggy rolls to a dog I liked!'

The ship lurched again and Juniper looked at the bucket in his hands.

'Nothing some fresh air won't fix,' said Thaddeus persuasively.

With another belch, Juniper struggled out of his hammock, staggered his way up the steps and disposed of the pail on the deck. He was rewarded with a slap of sea spray and a whip of wind across his dimpled face. Thaddeus poked his head out alongside him and together they surveyed the deck.

'Um … I say, old chap, maybe we should just stay put,' Juniper said, looking up at the dark clouds.

Thaddeus knew his friend was hearing the same fearsome thunderclaps that seemed to encourage the waves to rock the ship more vigorously with their enormous white-flecked fingers. Each time, the *Black Wyddah* tipped a little further sideways, getting perilously closer to capsizing.

'Yes, I think we should just stay put,' Juniper said, hurriedly withdrawing. 'Molly's probably safer where she is … Then there's Snitch …' When Thaddeus grabbed him by the arm, he protested, 'Think about it, old chap. Snitch could be about, then he'd tell Dibbers, and, well …'

Finally, Juniper ran out of excuses.

'Pfft, Snitch won't be about,' said Thaddeus. 'This wind would rip him to shreds – which would be no more than he deserves.' He pointed at the drenched crew as they battled the wind and wrested the sails. 'I doubt anyone will even notice if we sneak out of here.'

Juniper was still hesitant. 'How do you suppose we get from here to the ship's hatch?'

'Same way as the crew. Follow me!'

With that, he leapt onto the deck, grabbed hold of the tied rope and, clutching it tightly, pulled himself along it. A wave smashed over him, dragging his feet from beneath him. He froze with fear, remembering what it was like beneath that cold frothy water. Maybe this wasn't such a good idea after all. Maybe the sea would claim him for herself.

He lay there for a second, gripped by terror, before regaining his footing. Finally, his toes found the hatch to the belly of the *Wyddah*. Within seconds, he'd wriggled through the opening with only his tousled head left poking out.

'Flip!' exclaimed Juniper, the word immediately carried away on the shrieking air. He grasped hold of the sodden rope and took a tentative step out of the sea chest. Thaddeus beckoned him impatiently. If Juniper didn't hurry up, they would most certainly be discovered.

One look at the monstrous waves preparing to crash on the deck made Juniper forget his caution. He scurried across the space between the sea chest and the hatch, and Thaddeus grabbed his arm and dragged him below.

CHAPTER NINE

THE SEA WITCH

J uniper was heaving again, this time because of the salty water he'd just swallowed.

'That wasn't so bad, was it?' Thaddeus said, thumping Juniper's back to help him dislodge a surprising amount of ocean. Then he looked around them at the dim space. 'It's like a maze down here. Which way should we go?'

Juniper shrugged miserably.

'This way, I think,' said Thaddeus, deciding on his left.

They stumbled along, deeper into the belly of the dark, groaning ship. They quickly worked out that if they held both arms out and supported themselves on the passage walls, they could walk almost without staggering.

'Why do you suppose Silver doesn't want us down here?' Thaddeus asked, eyeing the dim passages that led off in different directions, some with grubby closed doors. 'Remember when he was chasing me – he got extra angry when he thought I might come below. And then he goes and brings Molly down here ... it doesn't make sense.'

Juniper shrugged again. Thaddeus saw that his eyes were watering, probably with the effort of keeping his seasickness under control.

'Let's look in here,' said Thaddeus, stopping so suddenly at a closed door that Juniper bumped into the back of him.

Thaddeus pushed open the door. A bellow of snores and a rumble of bottom burps greeted them from a line of sleeping pirates in swaying hammocks. Thaddeus closed the door in disgust and they tiptoed away. Not that they really needed to tiptoe. The creaking of the ship's hull as she battled with the sea was loud enough to cover their footsteps.

They'd almost neared the end of the passage when Thaddeus felt Juniper tugging on his sleeve. 'Listen,' he whispered anxiously.

Thaddeus cocked his head to the side and strained to hear what Juniper was hearing. A flap of wings and a smothered squawk greeted his ears. It was coming from the opening to a set of steps that led to the level beneath them and getting closer with each second.

'Snitch!' hissed Thaddeus. 'He'll have Dibbers onto us in no time and then we'll never find Molly. Quick, in here.'

He flung open a door to their left – fortunately a storage cupboard. He closed the door quietly, leaving only the smallest of gaps to see through. They watched tensely from the squishy cupboard, waiting for Snitch to pass them by. They didn't have to wait long.

Dibbers' parrot flew up the steps onto their level, and attempted to fly in a straight line along the passage, but the rocking of the ship caused the walls to smack him firmly in the beak, sending him wobbling wildly off course. This continued the whole length of the passage and Thaddeus had to cover his mouth with his hand to stop his laughter escaping.

He didn't open the cupboard door wide until he was sure it was safe.

'Phew, that was close,' said Juniper, wiping a bead of sweat from his brow. 'It would have been starvation for the next month. We'd likely have ended up using the sea chest as our coffin.'

'This way,' said Thaddeus, moving briskly in the direction Snitch had just come from.

He had taken only four steps when the rolling of the ship caused the door of the cupboard they'd been hiding in to fly open. Buckets, brushes and brooms fell out with a loud clatter. Both boys froze instantly.

The door to the pirates' hammock room at the other end of the passage bashed open and a club-headed face poked out. Bleary eyes instantly focused on the startled boys.

'Oi! What be ye doin' down 'ere?' the pirate yelled.

Another head, and then another, poked out of the doorway next to him.

Thaddeus didn't hang around. 'Come on!' he said, dragging Juniper by his sleeve.

They slid down the ladder steps to the next level faster than any fireman down a pole, and landed in another long lantern-lit passage much like the one they'd just left.

'Which way?' asked Juniper anxiously, looking at the line of doors and side passages. Footsteps thundered overhead, followed by the sound of someone tripping over the contents of the cupboard and an alarmed squawk.

'Doesn't matter — let's just not get caught,' said Thaddeus, sprinting away from the ladder.

Juniper, surprisingly, kept up with Thaddeus

as he darted left, then right, then left again, and down another ladder to a lower level.

'How big do you suppose this ship is?' Thaddeus puffed, finally slowing outside the next door they came to. He opened it and he and Juniper squeezed inside.

'Big,' answered Juniper. 'I say, I think we lost them.' He bent over, supporting his hands on his knees, and tried to catch his breath. The green tinge of seasickness had been replaced by the red of exertion.

'And lost ourselves,' said Thaddeus.

He looked around. It was darker in this room, with only a few sparse lanterns for illumination. It gave him the feeling that the *Wyddah* had swallowed them completely. It was also strangely quiet, almost as if they were below the surface of the storm and the threatening waves. He shivered. He didn't like it. It felt unnatural and he'd sooner just leave. But they needed somewhere to hide for a while.

He squinted into the gloom. The room seemed to go on forever, as if it took up one whole side of the ship with no dividing walls. Unfortunately there didn't seem to be any obvious hiding places. He took a step forwards and his foot landed in knee-deep water.

'The floor's all wet! I hope the ship hasn't sprung a leak.' He looked around worriedly.

'I expect the roughness of the storm broke one of those,' Juniper said, pointing through the gloom to some shadowy hulks that looked like large barrels. 'Probably the pirates' drinking water. I say, look at all this sand. They must have brought it down here to hold the barrels in place, but one of them tipped over with the lurching of the ship.'

Juniper's observation set Thaddeus's mind at ease. It made perfect sense.

He stepped out of the shallow water by the door and up onto a sandy bank, making for the barrels. They looked like they offered the best place to hide down here. Juniper quickly followed.

When they got closer, Thaddeus halted, surprised. They weren't water barrels he was looking at. They were rocks, embedded deep in the sand.

'I don't like it down here,' said Juniper suddenly, edging close to Thaddeus. 'I think we should go back.'

'What and be punished some more by Silver? I don't think so, Jupe. We came to find Molly, remember.

'Something doesn't smell right down here. And I'll tell you something else,' Juniper looked around worriedly, then bent to rub his knees, 'I don't think this is drinking water. It's salty – I can feel it stinging my knees. And look where we're standing. It's weird. It's like we're on a beach, and that water is the sea. I'm telling you, something smells fishy.'

'Like a cabin full of sleeping pirates?' Thaddeus joked. But he was covering his own concern. Juniper was right. If he didn't know for sure that he was on a ship, he'd think he was standing in the middle of a very gloomy and isolated beach.

'Thaddeus, let's go –'

Both boys froze as Juniper's words were gobbled up by a strange sound. It resembled someone sucking the dregs from a glass through a giant straw. It was followed by the sound of something slithering along the sand towards them.

They were not alone. There was something else in the room. And it was coming straight for them.

'W-w-what was th-that?' stuttered Juniper, his whole body wobbling with fear.

Thaddeus whipped a lantern from its hook on the wall and held it up high. The light didn't penetrate very far into the shadows, and when the noise came again he found himself backing up with Juniper.

'I-I think w-we sh-should go NOWWWW!' Juniper's words ended on a scream.

A huge shadow had appeared on the wall, sending both boys spinning around to peer anxiously into the gloom behind them. Thaddeus could feel the thump, thump of his heart hammering in his chest.

The shadow disappeared.

'W-w-what is it?' Juniper was almost incoherent with fear.

Thaddeus squinted into the dimness outside the lantern's circle. He couldn't see anything, but he knew from the icy fingers of fear crawling up his neck that something was out there. Something that was staring hungrily straight at him.

'L-let's g-g-go!' squeaked Juniper.

He began edging with the speed of a tortoise towards the knee-deep water and the door. Thaddeus edged with him, his eyes never leaving the shadows. He daren't turn his back on whatever was watching them.

He felt rather than saw Juniper lift his leg ready to step down into the water from the sandbank. A slithery, sloshing movement caused him to plant his foot firmly back on the sand.

'I-i-it's in th-the w-w-water.'

Thaddeus shone the light into the black pool.

Nothing moved. Nothing shivered. Nothing sprang out at them.

Then a splash some distance away sent a ripple of water towards them. Thaddeus and Juniper stood glued to the spot with terror. The ripple grew and became a wave, washing their way. Juniper made a sound somewhere between a sob and a gasp. Thaddeus silently begged his bladder to remain intact.

Both leapt back from the water's edge and crashed straight into a wall of dripping scale and slime. A wall that hadn't been there a moment ago.

Before either of them could turn to see what it was, the wall moved and they toppled onto their backs. The lantern dropped and shattered. The oil seeped out, forming a small pool, which quickly caught alight, brightening the room considerably.

Thaddeus and Juniper found themselves looking up into the seething eyes of an enormous creature with the head and upper body of a woman, her torso covered in shells and barnacles, and the lower body of a snake. *No, not a snake, a fish*, corrected Thaddeus as the tail, which had caused the rippling wave, slithered out of the water. The creature was blocking their exit, writhing back and forth like the tail of an angry cat. Thaddeus had a dreadful feeling that this was the 'she' that Skip had accidentally mentioned. But who was she? *What* was she?

The creature didn't say anything, just watched them as a hawk watches a mouse in a field. Thaddeus knew without a flicker of doubt that he and Juniper were in big trouble.

He climbed slowly to his feet and Juniper followed. The creature hissed. Juniper whimpered and shuffled sideways into the limited protection of Thaddeus's body.

'Just keep still,' Thaddeus whispered through gritted teeth.

The creature rose higher on her tail until she towered over the two terrified boys. Then in one quick swoop, she descended until her face was level with theirs. Thaddeus flinched, closing his eyes. He felt the disturbance of air fan his cheeks and smelt the overwhelming stench of rotten fish on a hot day.

When he didn't feel the pain of razor-sharp teeth slicing through him, he opened his eyes one at a time. The monster was still hovering inches from his face, her open mouth forming words. Thaddeus stared. Was that a finger caught between her upper incisors?

'So you have come to steal it,' she said, her

voice a rasping hiss.

Thaddeus felt Juniper slump against him and knew that his friend's legs had buckled.

'S-s-steal w-w-hat?' Juniper blubbered. 'W-w-we w-were j-just leaving a-actually.'

'You lie, boy,' hissed the creature. 'You have come for it! You have come for the Sea Witch's box.'

Her forked tongue darted around her teeth, dislodging the finger-thing and dragging it back to the depths of her throat. She swallowed hungrily.

'We don't know any Sea Witch,' said Thaddeus with a trembling voice.

'Lies! All lies! I know it is so. For *I* am the Sea Witch and you have come to steal the box from me.'

The Sea Witch swiped her tail forwards and uncoiled it to reveal a box the size of a small suitcase. It was dripping wet, encrusted with barnacles, and the locks that fastened the lid to the base were so rusted that they looked like fat blobs of sucked chocolate.

Thaddeus stared at the box and felt an overwhelming urge to open it. Juniper must have felt it too, for his legs had steadied and he was suddenly moving forwards, his nose sniffing the air.

As quickly as she had produced the box, the Sea Witch whisked it away, leaving Thaddeus feeling desperate. He had to have that box. He had to open it and take what was inside. He didn't know why, he just felt that he must. The Sea Witch was right. He *had* come to steal the box.

'Bring it back,' whined Juniper.

'THIEVES!' shrieked the Sea Witch, rising to her full height and swaying like a cobra ready to strike.

The movement dissipated the box's allure. As though waking from a deep sleep, Thaddeus realised they were in danger. If they didn't run now, it would be too late. Much too late!

'MOVE!' he yelled at Juniper, who was still looking forlornly at the space where the box had been.

The Sea Witch lunged. Thaddeus pulled Juniper out of the way and her face smashed into the sand where they'd just been standing.

Thaddeus ignored the desire for the box that was coursing through his veins and jumped over the tail that shot whip-like towards them. Juniper wasn't so limber. He tripped over the tail and fell headfirst onto the sand.

As Thaddeus bent to help him up, the Sea Witch swooped towards them again. Thaddeus scooped up a handful of sand and threw it straight into her eyes. The Sea Witch screamed and raised her hands to her face, rubbing at the grit that scratched her eyeballs.

'Come on,' urged Thaddeus, pulling Juniper up and dragging him to the door. He reached it and flung it open.

The Sea Witch heard, and screamed with fury. Half-blinded, she plunged towards the splashing sound of the boys' feet.

Thaddeus pushed Juniper through the opening and, with the breath of the beast on his neck, dived through after him. His heart beat a staccato in his chest and his mind chanted, *We're not going to make it … we're dead … so very dead.*

He landed heavily in the passage and rolled, his arms coming up protectively around his head. His eyes were clamped shut as he waited for the first painful slice of those angry teeth. When nothing happened, he gingerly opened one eye.

The Sea Witch hadn't followed them through, although not for want of trying. She was lunging furiously at the doorway, but it was as if there was an invisible barrier blocking her way. A spell was clearly in place.

Thaddeus felt relief flood through him. He jumped up and smoothed down his rumpled and sandy shirt, and grinned at the Sea Witch. 'What's the matter, you big fat slimy fish? Can't get out of your bowl. Ha! What a shame. All brawn and no brains. I'll be seeing you – not!'

He kicked the door shut, blocking out the Sea Witch's writhing angry form, and pulled a still dazed Juniper to his feet by his shirtsleeve. He dragged him shakily up the ladder to the next level, where he cautiously poked his head through the hatch, expecting at any moment to feel a pirate's calloused hands wrap around his throat.

He needn't have worried. The storm seemed to have increased in fervour, drawing all hands onto the *Wyddah*'s drenched deck.

Thaddeus made his way along the passage to the next ladder, panting at the extra effort it took to lug Juniper with him. Juniper seemed oblivious to where they were going. He kept looking longingly over his shoulder, and Thaddeus was certain that if he hadn't been there to hold him back, Juniper would have returned to the Sea Witch's lair.

'Keep going, Jupe,' he said, feeling annoyed.

It wasn't as if Thaddeus himself wasn't still feeling the strong pull of the box. It was just that he had stronger self-control. Besides, he knew that to go back for the box now would be useless. They just had to wait until there was another opportunity to take it. And he intended to make sure there was one.

'I need to go back, old chap. I must have that box,' Juniper whined, interrupting Thaddeus's thoughts.

'Course we'll go back, Jupe, it's just about timing. We need a plan to get around the Sea Witch. Then the box will be ours. Besides, we really ought to find Molly.'

***

With all the pirates up on deck battling the storm, the boys were free to explore the various passages and rooms below decks. They cautiously opened door after door and peeked inside. But none held Molly.

Juniper's stomach set up a disgruntled rumbling, but he didn't seem to notice. Nothing, it seemed, was going to distract him from the box.

'What do you suppose a Sea Witch is?' he asked, opening another door and peeking absently inside.

'I don't know,' said Thaddeus. 'Not a mermaid, surely? I didn't think they were so ugly. Did you see her hair? It looked exactly like squid tentacles, and then there were all those scales …

and did you see that finger stuck in her teeth? I'm sure it was a finger … ugh! I'll tell you something though – I reckon she's the reason Silver didn't want us coming below. Think about it, Jupe. He doesn't want us finding that box and using it to free ourselves.'

Juniper stopped and looked blankly at Thaddeus. 'I'm not sure how that box can free us.'

It was Thaddeus's turn to look blank. 'What do you mean? The box holds power … I thought you felt it too. Silver knows that. That must be why he's trapped the Sea Witch on the *Black Wyddah*. I'd say Noxious is involved too,' he continued darkly. 'Only a powerful spell could trap a monster like that.' He moved to the next door, Juniper trailing after him. 'Anyway, I reckon Silver plans on using the box to free Pepperjack from wherever he's imprisoned. It'll work too, because that box holds more power than any human has ever touched. I could feel it in my fingers. If I can just get that box, I can fix everything … *change everything* … like my parents …'

His voice trailed off as he thought of all the things he could do if only he had the box.

Juniper's blankness was replaced with confusion. 'I say, old chap, you've got it all wrong. The box doesn't hold power, it holds food. The kind of food that people only get to dream about.' He smiled dreamily and Thaddeus saw dimples appear in his cheeks.

He looked at Juniper in disbelief. He couldn't be serious. The lack of breakfast this morning had obviously affected him more than Thaddeus had thought. He'd have to get some food into him before they could discuss the matter further.

'I wonder where the galley is? Maybe we should get something to eat before we find Molly,' he suggested.

'I'm not feeling hungry for anything that might be in a ship's galley,' said Juniper.

Thaddeus stopped walking and stared at him. Usually Juniper leapt towards food with gusto. Something clearly wasn't right.

'Are you still feeling sick?' he asked.

'It's not that,' sighed Juniper. 'I really can't get my mind off that box. Nothing seems appetising after smelling what was in it.'

Thaddeus felt his jaw drop open. Juniper *was* serious. He really thought the box held food. It didn't make sense.

'I couldn't smell anything except that old Witch's breath, and I hardly think the stink of rotting fish would make you go off any other food,' he said.

But Juniper wasn't to be dissuaded and Thaddeus started to feel worried. What if Juniper was right and he wasn't?

'What did the box smell like then?' he asked.

'Well, that's just it, old chap, I don't really know.' Juniper's brow furrowed. 'I feel like it's something I've tasted before, but I can't recall what it was. I'm not even sure it's exactly food.' He scratched his head, clearly puzzled. 'All I know is I'm hungry for it, and I absolutely won't be satisfied until I can have what's inside that box.'

Thaddeus nodded. That part he understood, because he felt exactly the same.

'Well, there's only one way we'll know for sure. We'll have to steal the box,' he said decidedly.

Juniper brightened considerably and immediately spun around to return to the Sea Witch's prison. Thaddeus grabbed the back of his shirt.

'First things first, Jupe. If we're gonna get the box, we have to have a plan. We won't get past the Sea Witch without one. Her teeth were like razors, remember. And we've already made her angry. She'd be happy to take a chunk out of both of us.' He looked down at his arm, comparing it to Juniper's. 'Well, she'd take a chunk out of you, Jupe, and maybe use me as a toothpick.'

At Thaddeus's words Juniper looked like a big pink balloon that had been blown up one second, and popped the next.

'So what is your plan, old chap?' he asked dully.

Thaddeus didn't have a plan – yet.

'Come on,' he said instead. 'We really need to find Molly.'

But as they rounded the next corner, they heard a familiar squawk pierce the air.

'Snitch again!' said Thaddeus. 'He sounds close. What does he think he is – a sentry?'

Juniper dived straight through the nearest doorway and Thaddeus followed, neither boy stopping to consider what might be on the other side.

'Quick, shut the door – quietly,' hissed Thaddeus.

As Juniper did so, Thaddeus heard a rusty creak behind him. He spun around and felt his jaw hit his chest when he realised the noise came from a giant ornate birdcage swinging on an unoiled chain. But it wasn't the enormous cage that caused his eyes to bulge. *It was what was inside.*

CHAPTER TEN

OUTSMARTING A WIZARD

'Molly?' whispered Thaddeus, astounded.

Molly's head jerked around and her strained eyes took in Thaddeus and Juniper. A frightened look flitted across her face and she said just one word: 'Hide!'

Thaddeus recognised her tone from when she'd told him to stop wobbling the spider's web. He grabbed Juniper's sleeve, darted across the room, pushed him into a large cupboard and sprang in after him.

'LET ME OUT!' yelled Molly, giving the cage a fierce shake to cover the creaking of the cupboard door as Thaddeus shut it, leaving only a peephole gap.

At first Thaddeus thought Molly had gone mad, telling them to hide and then yelling to no one at all. It was a reasonable assumption when he calculated that she'd been gone for a long time and had quite possibly been locked in that cage for all of it.

The bang of a glass being slammed down on a table and an audible curse changed his mind, and through the gap in the door he noticed a doorway through to another cabin. It seemed that he and Juniper had chosen the very worst door to hide behind. They had just entered the wizard's quarters.

'What's going on, old chap?' whispered Juniper. 'I can't see a thing. What's Molly saying?'

'Shhh!' said Thaddeus, inching over a little to allow Juniper to share the view.

Both boys immediately froze. Noxious had appeared in the connecting doorway, his wand raised. His eyes zipped around the room before focusing again on Molly.

'I warned you – no noise,' he said, and strolled towards the cage with his wand still raised.

Thaddeus tightened his legs ready to spring. Wand or no wand, he wasn't about to watch this filthy wizard torment Molly. Not when it was his fault that she was trapped on the *Wyddah*. His calves quivered with tension, and only relaxed when he realised that Molly was shaking her head to warn him to remain hidden, rather than in denial as Noxious was assuming.

'You dare to tell me no?' Noxious tapped the cage with his wand and muttered a word. A fat blue bucket appeared, squashed between Molly and the inside of the cage's bars.

'Tell me where the knife is,' he demanded.

'I don't have it,' Molly said wearily, resting her head against the bars. 'What do you want it for anyway?'

Noxious was silent for a moment, then said, 'There is only one knife in this world that is invisible to the eye. Did you know that, girl? Such a knife can cut through anything, even unseen bonds – but in order to work it must be given, not taken.'

Molly shook her head again, but Noxious wasn't watching. He'd raised his bandaged hand and Thaddeus could see that even though the dressing looked new it was already stained a painful red.

'See this hand? It shows that I am bound by a promise that nothing, *nothing*, can undo. Except perhaps your knife. Now show it to me. I know you have it.'

'Whatever you promised, you should keep it,' said Molly.

Noxious's expression became thunderous.

'You know nothing. Some promises are forced upon a person, leaving them with no choice but to agree. Now give me the knife!'

'I will never give it to you,' said Molly fiercely.

'We shall see. If there is one thing I know, girl, it is that everyone has their limit.' He tapped the cage again. '*Graviter!*' A cruel smile spread across his nasty face. 'No mess now.'

Thaddeus glimpsed Molly's knuckles tightening around the bars before the cage started spinning dizzily.

'Five minutes ought to make you more generous,' Noxious said silkily, and he turned and strode back into the other room.

Thaddeus, filled with fierce hatred, watched him go. Then his eyes flicked back to Molly. She was vomiting noisily into the bucket.

'Oh, I can't watch,' moaned Juniper, clutching his empty stomach and moving away from the crack in the door.

Noxious turned in the doorway and raised his wand. '*Zippit.*'

Molly's heaving didn't cease, it just became silent.

Thaddeus's hands tightened into fists. He had just made up his mind to give that stinker Noxious a piece of his mind when someone bashed on the door to the passage.

'Enter,' said Noxious.

Silver, looking wetter than the sea surrounding them, entered and stood breathlessly just inside the room. 'Be ye havin' any luck yet?' he asked the wizard.

'I just need a little more time to convince her,' Noxious snarled.

'Well, best be leavin' her for a bit. We be havin' a bigger problem. Snitch be tellin' Dibbers the boys is escaped down the hatch. We need ye to use yer magic to find 'em again.'

'It will have to wait,' snapped Noxious. 'Have you forgotten that our imperative is to get the knife?'

Silver glowered at the wizard. 'No, I bain't be forgettin',' he said darkly. 'The sooner ye be unbindin' yerself from Pepperjack, the sooner ye be leavin' this ship. And then I'll be its best Captain.' His bushy beard separated, showing a wide grin. 'Pepperjack only be as feared as he is with yer help and magic. But best *ye* bain't be forgettin' what it means for ye iffen we lose the lads. A promise only be stretchin' so far, Noxious – and yer hand looks like ye be stretchin' it to the very limit.'

Noxious immediately hid his bleeding hand in his robe. 'Leave me! The children won't get far. I'll see to them shortly.'

'I knew Noxious was up to something,' whispered Thaddeus to Juniper. 'That hand isn't bleeding for no reason.'

Silver turned to Molly, who was still vomiting into the bucket. 'Best be givin' 'im what he wants, girly.' And he clomped out of the cabin.

As soon as Silver had gone, Noxious tapped the cage and said, '*Desisto!*' The cage stopped spinning, and he tapped the door and muttered something else, but Thaddeus didn't hear what it was because Juniper chose that exact moment to sneeze.

Noxious spun around and stared at the cupboard. 'Well, well, well, what kind of mice do we have in the cupboard?' he drawled, a nasty grin on his face.

He took two strides to the door and reached out his hand at the same time Thaddeus smashed open the door. It smacked the wizard hard in the face, unbalancing him. He dropped his wand. Thaddeus leapt out of the cupboard and pounced on it, then pointed it directly at Noxious.

He tried not to notice his hand trembling as he said, 'Don't move or I'll ... I'll say a spell!'

The wizard dropped his hand from his injured face and laughed. 'You think you can manage a wand, boy?' He took a menacing step forward.

'*GRAVITER!*' yelled Thaddeus, repeating the spell he'd heard Noxious use on Molly.

The wizard's feet were whipped out from under him and he flew up into the air upside down and began spinning wildly around the cabin. His head hit the side of the cage and the blow knocked him out immediately.

'I say – that was a lucky shot!' Juniper came out of the cupboard, his eyes bulging as he watched the upside-down, unconscious wizard zoom around the cabin.

Thaddeus tucked the wand into his belt and ran to the cage. Molly was still slumped over the bucket. He rattled the door. It was locked.

'Juniper, see if you can find the key,' he ordered.

Juniper went through to the next cabin and Thaddeus heard him rifling through objects on Noxious's desk. 'I can't see a key, old chap – but he's got all sorts here. What a messy fellow.'

Thaddeus followed to help and realised Juniper was no longer looking for the key. Instead he was staring at a scrap of torn paper in his hand.

'I say, I think you should see this,' he told Thaddeus, his voice hushed. 'I think it's from Pepperjack's memoir!'

Juniper handed the piece of paper to Thaddeus and both boys sat on the floor of the wizard's cabin to watch the scene that unfolded before them. Thaddeus felt a twinge of guilt at leaving Molly locked in the cage, but told himself the fragment from the memoir might hold vital information. Besides, she wasn't vomiting any more, not since Noxious's spell had worn off and the cage had stopped spinning.

The scene showed a dark night, and Noxious and Captain Pepperjack were in a small boat racing across the ocean towards a dark island. Noxious had his wand raised and it seemed to be his magic that was propelling the boat. Neither pirate nor wizard spoke, until the boat slowed alongside some cliffs at the far end of the island.

'There,' said Pepperjack, pointing to a dark hole in the rock face.

Noxious silently manoeuvred the boat through the mouth of the cave and Thaddeus heard its bottom scrape against pebbles just before it came to a halt. Noxious stepped out, followed by Pepperjack.

'*Ignis*,' said Noxious, and a ball of flame shot out of his wand and hung in the air high above him. It illuminated every inch of the cave, and the boys saw the Sea Witch in a crevice at the back.

The light brought her snaking forwards.

'So, you have come,' she hissed.

Pepperjack stepped forwards, unafraid. 'Ye knew Pepperjack would come. Ye be having some information I be wanting.'

'There is nothing I would share with you, Pepperjack. You have committed many crimes and now you shall be punished for your murderous actions.'

'That be *Captain* Pepperjack to ye!' the pirate snarled.

The Sea Witch shrieked and lunged at him, but she was so focused on Pepperjack that she forgot to keep an eye on Noxious. He touched the tip of his wand to the tiny tattoo of the *Black Wyddah* that sat behind his ear. His hand was trembling and blood was seeping through the bandages. He muttered something and part of the tattoo split away from his skin, floating into the air like a scrap of ash.

'*Impello signum*,' he said, and the fragment stuck itself behind the Sea Witch's ear.

She screamed as if she'd been burnt and clawed at the mark, but it stuck on as firmly as if it had been tattooed there.

'Ye be bound to Pepperjack now, and there be no undoing it,' gloated the pirate.

'I cannot be bound to you – I have not signed your wicked contract,' the Sea Witch shrieked.

Pepperjack laughed. 'Ye be bound alright. Your magic is no match for that which protects Pepperjack – not this time.'

'Traitor!' yelled the Sea Witch, lunging towards Noxious.

'Enough!' Pepperjack's order snapped the Sea Witch upright and held her motionless. 'Just look at ye. The Queen of the Seven Seas and a wizard, both at Pepperjack's command!' His laughter bounced off the walls of the cave, mocking both the Sea Witch and Noxious. 'And now, Witch, ye'll tell Pepperjack what he be needing to know.'

'You have but one question,' hissed the Sea Witch. 'You want to know the whereabouts of the most sought-after treasure.'

Her tail uncoiled and flicked around to rest in front of Pepperjack. Suddenly the scene became fuzzy, like a television channel that isn't properly tuned.

'What happened?' demanded Thaddeus.

'I think the page got damaged when it was crumpled up on Noxious's desk,' said Juniper. 'I say – look, it's coming back.'

The memoir scene refocused – still in the cave, but Pepperjack was missing and Noxious was arguing with the Sea Witch.

'I can't release you!' he yelled. 'What is done cannot be undone.' He pointed his wand hand towards the back of the cave, which was in darkness again. The bandages on his hand had disappeared and the boys could see deep cuts all over his skin, every one oozing blood. 'You have imprisoned Pepperjack, but you cannot be freed from his contract unless you kill him.'

'I cannot harm him,' spat the Sea Witch. 'The contract prevents me. And I will not release him for then he would kill me. It is as you say: what is done cannot now be undone.'

'Then you are bound to the *Wyddah* along with the rest of her crew,' Noxious said. 'Until we can work out a way...'

The memoir turned fuzzy again. Thaddeus desperately smoothed out the creases at the bottom of the fragment, but there was only one more bit to see. It showed Noxious ripping the page out of Pepperjack's memoir.

'So Noxious does know where Pepperjack is,' said Thaddeus, 'and he's determined not to set him free.' When Juniper looked doubtful, he added, 'Look at the facts, Jupe. He tried to kill me when the pirates brought me on board. And then he sent me to Safe Harbour thinking I wouldn't come back. He looked surprised when I did come back, and with Molly too. All along he's been trying to stop the pirates getting what they need to find their Captain and bring him back.'

'But you bringing back Molly worked out for him,' Juniper said. 'She has a knife that he wants.'

'Yes, but that's his only piece of luck. And now he's trying to cover his tracks. He must have placed a spell on Stubbs so he could get his hands on Pepperjack's memoirs and rip out this page so no one else could find out where the Captain is imprisoned. Jupe, we need to get off this ship and fast before Silver comes back.' Thaddeus carefully rolled up the memoir page and placed it in his pocket. 'Now we just need to find the key to Molly's cage.'

After another ten minutes of searching, it became clear that they weren't going to find it. Or maybe there wasn't a key at all …

Thaddeus returned to the cage, and felt another twinge of guilt when he saw Molly lying on its floor, pale and limp.

'Molly, do you remember how Noxious locked you in? Did he use a spell?'

Molly lifted her head and whispered, 'Wand … *Libero*…'

'Okay,' Thaddeus said, ducking his head as

the still unconscious wizard circled past. 'Move away from the door.'

Molly shuffled slowly backwards and Thaddeus pointed the wand at the cage. '*Libero!*'

Nothing happened.

'*LIBERO!*' he yelled and gave the door a sharp tap with the wand.

The lock exploded off the cage with a loud bang and shot straight into the wand, snapping it in half.

Juniper came hurrying from the adjoining cabin to see what had caused the explosion. 'I say, old chap, that is bad luck. We could have used the wand to help us get off the *Wyddah*.'

Thaddeus dropped the broken wand to the floor and kicked it out of his way. Then he reached into the cage to help Molly out.

Once she had taken a few wobbling steps around the cabin to get the feeling back in her legs, she stared hard at Thaddeus and Juniper. 'Why did you come and get me after … after …' She couldn't finish.

Thaddeus knew it was partly guilt at tricking Molly into coming with him back to the *Wyddah*. But it was more than that too. There was something else that bound them together … something stronger.

'The same reason you didn't leave me in that web,' he said. 'It wouldn't have been right. You never leave a friend behind. *Never. No matter what.*'

Molly nodded grudgingly. 'So, we're friends then?'

Thaddeus and Juniper looked at each other before nodding.

'We're all we've got,' said Thaddeus. 'And now we need to get out of here. We can't risk being caught again – you especially, Molly. Not now Noxious is so desperate to get his hands on your knife.'

Molly nodded. 'But how? Where can we go? We're trapped on this ship.'

'I say, I don't suppose anyone will come looking for you?' asked Juniper hopefully.

Molly shook her head. 'The old woman who raised me is long dead. She told me she found me washed up on the beach in a basket, abandoned, so I guess I don't have any family.'

'There's a box we can use,' Thaddeus said. 'I just know it holds the power to set us free. We just need to get it –'

'I say, old chap, I told you before, that box doesn't –'

Thaddeus quickly cut Juniper off. 'Yes, yes, I know.' He needed Molly to believe the box held the power to set them free if he was going to successfully sell her his idea.

'Let's go and get it then!' she said, turning towards the door.

'But –' said Juniper.

'Jupe, it's okay,' Thaddeus whispered. 'Just think about the box. We need to get it from the Sea Witch. With that box in our hands, you'll be able to have all the food you want.'

It was a mean trick but it worked. Juniper's eyes took on a familiar glaze.

'The sea what?' asked Molly, pausing at the doorway.

Thaddeus sighed. 'The Sea Witch.' And he grudgingly filled her in on what dwelt in the belly of the *Wyddah*.

'What?' Molly said. 'You should have told me that to start with! I don't think it's a good idea going back there. What makes you think she'll be any happier to see you this time? You were lucky before, but next time you might not be.'

'We need to get the box from the Sea Witch,' Thaddeus said again, ignoring Molly as she shook her head vigorously. 'It's the only way. I know the box holds power and with it we'll be able to get away from the pirates and free Skip too.'

Molly was still doubtful. 'You don't even

know what's in the box. It could be a trick.'

'I vote yes,' said Juniper. His eyes were starry and he was licking his lips in anticipation. 'It's a grand idea.'

'That's two against one,' said Thaddeus. 'Majority rules.'

Molly stood firm, her lips in a tight line and her arms folded angrily across her chest.

'Look, if it's because you're afraid, you know, because you're a girl,' said Thaddeus sneakily.

'I'm not afraid of nothing,' said Molly. Her whole body was quivering with indignation. 'Alright, I'll come, but only to keep you two out of trouble. But I'm not going into the Witch's lair. I'll stand guard outside the door while you go and fetch the box. That's if you even can,' she added smugly.

Thaddeus ignored the jibe. He felt like he'd already won the argument. 'Suit yourself,' he said, careful to hide his triumphant smile.

When he got to the Sea Witch's barrier, he might even cluck like a chicken. See if that wouldn't change Miss Molly's mind.

***

With the plan all settled, Thaddeus quietly opened

the cabin door and peeked out. Except for the continual groaning of the wooden hull, and the occasional thump as the *Graviter* spell spun Noxious around the room, all was quiet.

'Follow me,' he whispered.

As they snuck along the passage, Thaddeus knew he had to keep his wits about him. It wouldn't do to run into any of the crew – or worse, Silver. He headed straight for the hatch that would take them to the lower levels and back to the Sea Witch's lair, all the while puzzling over how they were going to take the box from her. Molly had a valid point. The Sea Witch wasn't just going to hand it over. Still, this seemed an insignificant detail in light of what they stood to gain. Besides, the more Thaddeus thought about the box, the more the longing for it and its power pressed against him. Pretty soon he was telling himself that the box was as good as his.

With a triumphant smile on his face, he trod the last few steps to the door to the room that held the strange beach.

'This is it,' said Thaddeus. 'Are you sure you're not coming in, Molly?'

Molly shook her head and moved to a guard position beside the door. He knew she had her knife out. 'Yell if you need my help,' she said sarcastically.

'Let's go,' said Juniper, opening the door quickly. Thaddeus knew he was imagining all kinds of delicious things to eat inside the box.

'Here we go,' he muttered, following Juniper through the door and plunging straight into the knee-deep water.

The door swung silently shut and Thaddeus hesitated, blind until his eyes adjusted to the dim light. He blinked twice and focused on the bulky shape of Juniper, who was doing an impressive imitation of a statue. Thaddeus could have laughed. *Now* he decided to stand still.

Thaddeus moved two steps towards Juniper, then he too froze. The Sea Witch was waiting for them.

'You have come to steal the box,' she said in a voice laced with trickery.

Thaddeus held his tongue, fearful she might trip him up.

Juniper edged closer to him, his head shaking in what Thaddeus knew was a lie.

The Witch moved as fast as a streak of lighting until her face was only inches from theirs, her breath like acid on their cheeks. 'The bones never lie,' she hissed, scattering a handful of human knucklebones to the sand at Thaddeus's feet.

Thaddeus gulped. She'd known they would

return. They'd been doomed even before they left Noxious's quarters. They had just one hope – the Witch didn't seem to know about Molly. Thaddeus wondered if he should scream for help, but did he dare put Molly in danger again? What could she even do? The Sea Witch was big and powerful. Then again, Molly would make three – and she had the knife.

Thaddeus opened his mouth, but the shout died on his lips when the Witch uncoiled her fishlike tail to reveal the box. Thaddeus embraced the familiar feeling of power and smiled stupidly. Everything would be alright.

'We've come for the box and there's nothing you can do to stop us taking it,' he said cockily.

The Witch smiled. Unpleasantly, Thaddeus thought.

'Bigger, stronger and braver men have sought this box before you. And yet none of them have taken it,' the Sea Witch said.

She bent low and picked the box up in her hands. Juniper let out a moan. Thaddeus felt a tingling in his own hands and barely heard the Witch's voice through his haze of desire.

'Its attraction is strong,' she said. 'I feel it myself, and yet it is enough for me just to have the box within my keeping. But for humans it is not enough. You desire to open it, you itch to own what you think is inside. And yet when you do, it is always the same – you never find what you hoped for, you are never happy with what you get. It is always this way with humans.'

'You're lying,' said Thaddeus. He couldn't wrench his eyes from the box. He was so close to having everything he had ever dreamed of. He wouldn't have to worry about finding his mother's dreams. He could change everything. He could stop his father from leaving. Just two little steps and he would be touching it. Two tiny steps and he could prise it from those scaly hands.

His feet moved as if they had a mind of their own. From the corner of his eye, he noticed a hulking shadow. It was Juniper, moving too – but it didn't matter. The box was there. It was nearly his. He reached out a hand, and touched it.

The Sea Witch smiled beguilingly. Thaddeus smiled back and reached out his other hand. This was it – he could feel the power. He floated high on it and saw himself lifted from the sand. It was astonishing.

The air rushed against his face as he came back to land, then he felt the coldness of water … It doused his desire for the box immediately. Panic rushed over him as his eyes focused and he realised he was in the Witch's water.

But then the box took hold again, his thoughts glazed … and it didn't matter. He was stronger than the water, he was –

'THADDEUS! JUNIPER!'

The yell shattered his reverie like a rock breaking the ice on a frozen lake. He blinked and was able to see clearly again. The Sea Witch had him and Juniper wrapped in her coils.

Juniper was already up to his neck in inky water. With a hiss the Witch dragged him under.

The last thing Thaddeus saw before he too was swallowed by the sea was Molly on the sandbank screaming their names.

We're lost, thought Thaddeus, struggling futilely against the tightening coils. There was no help for them now. Molly was just as afraid of the water as he was.

CHAPTER ELEVEN

BARGAIN WITH A WITCH

Thaddeus heard the Sea Witch scream. Bubbles frothed around him, blinding him. The coils loosened and he felt something grab his arm — something else that had a tail like the Sea Witch. It shot Thaddeus and Juniper to the surface of the water and towards the shallows, where the waves lapped the sand.

Thaddeus choked and spluttered, clearing his lungs of salty water. He turned to his left and saw Juniper spluttering and coughing too. On his right was Molly. She was leaning towards him, her wet hair flopping around her now clean face.

'You've washed your face,' he said stupidly. His mind was still blurred from the effects of nearly drowning.

'And you've grown a tail,' added Juniper just as stupidly, before fainting and landing with a heavy thump onto the sand.

Thaddeus looked down. Sure enough, where Molly's legs should have been, there was a scaly fishy tail.

'What the heck is that?' he said, but the pieces suddenly fell into place. So that was the thing she'd been hiding from him in the rowboat from Safe Harbour. She didn't want to get wet because her legs would change to a fishy tail. He shuffled away from her without thinking.

Molly looked hurt. 'Oh, that's just great! I knew if I told you … I save your lives and you move away from me!'

'Molly, it's not that. It's just a shock, that's all.'

Thaddeus didn't have time to apologise further. The Sea Witch rose out of the water in front of them, hissing and writhing with anger. A ragged slash gaped from her shoulder to her elbow. Even as he watched, it began to congeal and heal.

'You are very persuasive, child,' said the Sea Witch through clenched teeth.

Molly shuffled back awkwardly, her tail dragging in the sand. She could neither walk nor swim right now, for her tail was slowly mutating back to two human legs.

Thaddeus supposed he could have run, but

he couldn't tear his eyes from Molly's changing tail-legs, and Juniper was still passed out on the sand.

Molly raised her knife against the Sea Witch. The Witch could clearly see it for she looked shocked.

'You have much to learn, little one. We never harm our own,' she said.

'I didn't know,' said Molly. 'I just wanted to save my friends and you wouldn't listen. Y-you gave me no choice.' The Sea Witch's face darkened and Molly's voice wavered, like a naughty child's before a scolding parent. 'I- I'm sorry. They shouldn't have tried to steal your box. But if you must know, they have good intentions. Thaddeus wants to use it to save Skip and kill Pepperjack, and –'

The Sea Witch hissed even louder and looked ready to strike. 'You dare speak of him? That monster who is the cause of me being chained to this ship!'

Thaddeus tore his eyes away from Molly's now fully formed legs and looked at the Sea Witch. She seemed angry enough that she might still drag them all down to the sea's inky depths, so he remained perfectly still and silent.

The only sound that punctuated the silence

was Juniper's groan as he returned to the land of the living.

'I say, what's going on?' he asked. He blinked blearily and looked from Thaddeus to Molly. His back was to the Sea Witch so he hadn't yet noticed her. 'I say, Molly, I had the strangest dream. You had a tail – fancy that!' He scrambled to his feet and looked around. 'Did we get shipwrecked?' Then his eyes latched onto the Sea Witch. 'Oh,' he said quietly and fell silent.

'I have come to a decision,' said the Sea Witch at last. 'You say that your intention is to be rid of Pepperjack. That is my intention also. Only then will I be free of the magic that binds me to his ship. So I have decided you shall not die – *yet*.'

She lowered herself into the water and beckoned them to follow her.

Thaddeus helped Molly, whose legs were still shaky, and together the three of them walked along the sandbank into the gloomiest part of the Witch's lair. The sand ended at a collection of rocks, and the Sea Witch surged out of the water and sat herself on one.

'*Revelare*,' she said, touching another rock beside her. The rock yawned sleepily, opening its mouth wide like a schoolroom locker. The Sea Witch plunged her hand inside it and pulled out a small corked bottle tied to a black leather cord.

'A gift for you, Thaddeus Bix. It will help in your quest. Keep her with you at all times, even when you leave her decks for dry land.'

The Sea Witch placed the cord around Thaddeus's neck, and her hand disappeared back into the rock.

'Her?' questioned Thaddeus. He brought the corked bottle that now hung in the centre of his chest up to his eyes for a closer inspection, and felt a thrill at what he saw. Inside the bottle was a tiny ship with billowing sails. On the side of her hull were written the words *Sea Cat*.

'I say, that's a grand gift.' Juniper's eyes were as bright as birthday candles on a cake. He licked his lips appreciatively and reached out his hand to the Sea Witch.

'For you, Juniper Rose – the Buccaneers Chart.'

She gave him a crumpled piece of parchment folded into a messy square. It had rough edges and was marked with ancient-looking brown stains. Juniper unfolded it, but it was completely blank.

'Is that it?' he asked in disbelief, looking from Thaddeus's ship to the piece of rubbish in his own hand.

'Use it well, Juniper Rose,' the Witch said. 'It will lead you to the things you most hunger for.'

Juniper stuffed the parchment in his pocket and glared at Thaddeus, who was still taking in every detail of his miniature ship.

The Sea Witch's hand entered the rock's mouth a third time and she placed an old dented spyglass into Molly's hands.

'Molly Mallou, this is Caspian's Eye. It will only show you what you truly need to see.'

Molly's face resembled Juniper's when she noticed that the end of the spyglass was cracked like a frozen web. It really wasn't hard to tell who the Sea Witch favoured. But unlike Juniper, Molly simply said, 'Thank you,' and shoved the broken spyglass into her tunic pocket.

'I say, old chap,' Juniper whispered to Thaddeus, 'I think she must like you more.'

Thaddeus ignored him and looked at the Witch. 'Is that it? What about the box?'

The Sea Witch's face contorted with rage. 'The box is mine,' she hissed. 'It always has been and it always will be!'

'Okay then, what about a bargain?' Thaddeus said quickly. He wasn't about to give up so easily. 'How about you lend it to me on the promise that I return it to you?'

The Witch's eyes narrowed. He could see that her coils were tense, ready to spring.

'I say, that's a grand idea,' Juniper began.

'Silence!' said the Witch, reducing Juniper to a mumble. She looked at Thaddeus and when she spoke again her tone was slippery. 'You would bargain with a Witch, boy?'

'I would,' said Thaddeus, ignoring the tone.

The Witch brought the box from beneath her coils and laid it gently on the sand in front of her. Thaddeus felt the power swell within him and he knew he was on the right path.

'I will,' he repeated in a gush of emotion.

The Sea Witch pulled at a strand of her squid-tentacle hair. It came away from her scalp and lay wriggling in her palm. With her other hand, she took Thaddeus's and wound the squirming strand around and around and around their hands, binding them firmly together. Thaddeus wondered what on earth she was doing. He'd asked for the box, not a piece of her horrible hair. He wriggled his fingers within her scaly grip. He didn't like the feel of her rough skin, and the hair was like a cold eel holding him so tight it was beginning to hurt.

'A binding promise,' said the Witch. 'If you would bargain with a Witch, it must be so.'

Thaddeus nodded. He didn't really care. He just wanted her to hurry up and say her mumbo jumbo so he could get rid of the disgusting hair from around his hand and get the box. Once he had it, everything would be perfect.

'It is done,' said the Witch, unwinding the hair and removing her hand from his.

'What's done?' Thaddeus blinked and refocused his eyes and ears on the Witch. She'd been talking but he hadn't been listening.

She just smiled. A smile that made him think that something had just happened or was about to happen that he most certainly wouldn't like.

He looked at Molly. Her face was furious, her eyes blazing.

'Idiot … fool! You just agreed to set her free by burying the box, and you promised never to open it, you stupid twit,' she snapped. 'How do you suppose you can do one without the other?'

Thaddeus felt a tingle of unease. Surely he'd never agreed to *that*? He would need to open the box to get to the power it held, and without that power how could he free the Witch?

'And that's not all – we have to find some place called the Unknown Grave. So now we can't even go back to Safe Harbour. We have to go and find some grave on some island. How do you suppose we're going to get to this unknown grave? Did you think about that, genius? No!'

Molly ranted on, but Thaddeus was oblivious again because the Sea Witch was pushing her beloved box towards him.

'I have power now. Of course I can release her,' answered Thaddeus, smiling at Molly before picking up the box. 'At last,' he gasped, hugging it to his chest. His cheeks felt feverish.

Juniper moved forwards, pushing Molly roughly out of the way. 'I say, can I have a hold?'

Thaddeus didn't hear him. He was wrapped up in the moment, in the feelings coursing through him. His mind had never known such power, his body had never felt such strength. It didn't matter what he'd promised. After all, a promise wasn't valid if he couldn't remember making it. All he had to do now was open the box and all would be his.

He traced his fingers over the lid and its small groove, then stumbled when they came to the blobby latches that held the lid closed.

'I say, let me have a turn.' Juniper's face was flushed a discontented red.

Thaddeus didn't notice. He was mesmerised. His fingers were around the latch. They were lifting the rusted hinges upwards … Not long now … He was going to be powerful, so –

'AAAGGGGHHHHH!!'

Thaddeus dropped the box and grabbed his hand, a sob escaping his lips. He danced around holding the hand that not a moment before had been bound to the Witch's.

'What did you do? It feels terrible!' he choked out.

He hunched over, thinking he might be sick from the intensity of the pain. He couldn't even begin to describe it. He had never in his life felt anything so horrific. It was as if the skin of his hand was being peeled back layer by layer with agonising slowness.

'I did nothing,' said the Sea Witch. 'It was your own doing. The pain you feel is that of a promise being stretched tightly. The more you stretch that promise, the deeper it will cut. The pain should wear off soon, but let it be a lesson to you.'

Thaddeus looked at Molly. She was wearing a told-you-so look that went well with her sack-like tunic. Juniper was still staring longingly at the box, but Thaddeus's scream had kept him from leaping forwards to take it for himself.

'Molly, pass me your knife. I'll cut through the promise,' Thaddeus said.

Molly put her hand into her pocket, but didn't

withdraw it. 'I'm not sure you should,' she said slowly.

'Your friend is right,' hissed the Sea Witch. 'For every action, there is a consequence. If you cut yourself free from a binding promise, you will lose something of yourself. With each wrongdoing, your moral compass becomes damaged, until before you know it you are no longer travelling in the right direction.'

The Sea Witch's words reminded Thaddeus of how deeply his father's broken promise had hurt him and his mother.

When the pain in his hand had dulled, he bent to pick up the box again, careful to turn the latches away from him. It wouldn't do to give in to temptation a second time. He feared that if he did, it would kill him.

'You may go,' said the Sea Witch abruptly. 'But never forget,' her eyes bored into Thaddeus, 'a broken promise has grievous consequences.'

Thaddeus nodded. He had learnt his lesson. He wouldn't risk opening the box anytime soon. Besides, something more pressing was hammering against his mind. If he had promised to unchain the Sea Witch, he had to honour that promise or he'd feel that agony again. His hand might even drop off! This realisation particularly worried him because he had absolutely no idea how to free the Witch without opening the box.

'Come on,' he snapped at Molly and Juniper.

He made for the door and reached for its handle to yank it open and march out – only his face smacked against something hard that felt like glass. He realised it must be the invisible barrier that had kept the Sea Witch from chasing him and Juniper the first time. And now here it was keeping them from leaving.

He looked back at the Witch.

'That way is closed to you,' she said.

'I say, what do you mean closed?' asked Juniper, pushing against the barrier. It remained impenetrable.

'It wasn't closed before, so why now?' Thaddeus said irritably, and he kicked at the invisible glass. He was annoyed enough to break it, but the only thing he managed to do was to painfully dent his toes.

'Are there any other ways out?' asked Molly, ever practical.

'You are now bound to help me and you have accepted gifts that were long ago taken by the sea,' the Witch said. 'To keep them, you must go back through the sea.'

Her long bony finger pointed towards the

water lapping at the edge of the sand.

Thaddeus recoiled in horror at the thought of entering those inky depths. 'You can have your stinking gifts back,' he said, fumbling at the necklace holding the tiny ship in its bottle. He didn't think to offer the box.

'It is too late for that, Thaddeus Bix. You have willingly accepted your gifts. What is done cannot be undone. The only way you may leave now is through the water. The sea must have a chance to give up what is rightfully hers.'

'She doesn't have to give it up, she can keep it! Isn't that right, old chap?' Juniper tried his best to shove the piece of parchment back into the rock. But its mouth was clamped shut.

Thaddeus stared at the dark water. The thought occurred to him that it might be like a doorway. He might be able to just dunk his head under and come back up inside the *Wyddah*. That wouldn't be so bad.

'Where will we end up – you know, if we go through the water?' he asked. 'We don't want to land on top of a smelly pirate snoring in his hammock.'

The Witch didn't reply. She just pointed again at the inky water. 'It is the only way.'

'I'm not going in there – you know I can't

swim – it's a trick, isn't it – because of this stupid box. Here – have it back.'

Thaddeus reluctantly shoved the box at the Witch, but she waved it away with a lazy hand. So he took it back and clutched it to his chest.

'This is all your fault,' Molly told him. She looked as angry as a wasp.

'What are you whining about?' he said. 'At least you've got a tail to swim with. It's alright for you!'

'That's just it,' she snapped. 'I might have a tail but that doesn't mean I can use it.'

'I say, what's going on?' asked Juniper, scratching his head, clearly puzzled.

'Molly has a tail!' said Thaddeus in exasperation. 'It wasn't a dream. She's a … she's a … What are you, Molly? A mermaid?'

'A sea nymph,' answered the Witch when Molly didn't say anything. 'Mermaids can't change their tails to legs, whereas sea nymphs can adapt to the elements. Their bodies remain the same, only their legs change, becoming a tail, or vice versa.'

'Oh,' said Molly. It was obvious she hadn't known what she was. 'But it makes no difference. I've never been in the water until tonight, so I don't know how to swim.'

'Could have fooled me,' muttered Thaddeus.

'So what do we do then? My tummy's beginning to rumble, and we can't stay down here forever.' Juniper rubbed his belly for emphasis. 'Or maybe we can – that box still smells awfully good.'

Thaddeus hugged the box tighter and moved away a few steps. He didn't like Juniper's hungry lion look. He walked to the edge of the water and peered into it. If only he'd listened to Molly in the first place they most likely wouldn't be in this situation. It wasn't fair that the only way out of here was the way that most terrified him.

He looked back at Molly and Juniper, who were waiting for him to decide. He had got them into this mess. He would have to get them out of it.

'What do we do?' he asked the Sea Witch with dull resignation.

'Have faith,' she answered simply.

'It's alright for you to say – you've got gills,' muttered Thaddeus as he stepped into the water. His breath stuck in his throat, making him feel like he was already drowning.

Molly and Juniper didn't follow.

'Come on, Molly, you swam tonight when you rescued us. You know you can do it,' he said, trying to sound encouraging even though inside he felt sick.

Molly stayed where she was. 'But that's just it – I don't remember how. It just happened and I don't … I can't …'

'Jupe?' urged Thaddeus. They needed to hurry before his own spark of bravery was doused by the cold water.

'Come on, Molly, we need to stick together. You can hang on to me like a floaty,' joked Juniper.

His effort to lighten the mood fell flat. Thaddeus knew they were probably all thinking the same thing – that Juniper had the least to worry about. He could swim, which meant he was probably the only one who would make it out alive.

'Is there no other way?' Thaddeus asked again.

But his question was met with silence. The Sea Witch had disappeared.

Juniper led Molly to the water's edge and Thaddeus stepped back to take hold of her other hand. The water lapped around her feet and her legs began to merge together and take on a silvery hue.

'I can't stand,' she gasped.

Thaddeus and Juniper supported her and the three of them awkwardly shuffled further into the water.

'Keep going,' puffed Thaddeus. 'It's only knee deep here.'

One more step and the sandy floor gave way and they were plunged into deep water. They floated for a second, not realising what had happened. Then as the knowledge sank in, their bodies began to sink too.

'She lied, it's a trick!' spluttered Juniper. His head disappeared beneath the water as a panicked Molly locked her arms around him.

When Molly realised that Juniper was sinking with her, she let go of him and lunged for the only other thing that might keep her afloat. Thaddeus.

'Molly!' he gurgled, sucking in salty water and feeling himself going down.

He thrashed his legs, trying to dislodge her. Her tail was sinking them faster than any anchor. He couldn't shake her off unless he let go of the box. But he didn't want to let go of it.

They were all underwater now, and Molly became more frantic. Her hands tore at Thaddeus's clothes as she tried to claw her way back up to the surface.

Use your tail! Thaddeus screamed silently at her.

But Molly didn't know how. It seemed the tail would only work when she wasn't thinking of it.

And the terror in her eyes showed that she wasn't thinking of anything except drowning.

Thaddeus's shirt tore away in Molly's hands and she sank lower. She lunged at the nearest thing to her and her hands found the bottle that the Witch had given Thaddeus, which was still hanging around his neck.

The last thing Thaddeus saw before everything went black was the bottle opening and the tiny ship sliding out.

CHAPTER TWELVE

SHIP IN A BOTTLE

'He's dead.'

'Prod 'im then – see iffen he is.'

'You prod 'im, he's all wet.'

'What's about the fat one?'

'He's alright, so's the fish.'

'He's not dead, look at 'ims eyes.'

Thaddeus blinked wearily. His brain felt like a wet flannel and his nostrils were burning. He tried to remember. They'd been in the water … no, not in, *under* the water … Molly's tail … Juniper's face … a box. The thoughts floated around his mind like seaweed being tumbled in the ocean's waves. He opened his eyes wider and focused. He was back on the deck of a ship and he could hear voices … but whose voices, whose ship?

'Take it offen 'im.'

'You take it offen 'im!'

'Open it – it's got life in it. Quick, afore he wakes.'

Thaddeus sat up so suddenly he startled the owner of the voice into dropping the box. It landed neatly in Thaddeus's lap.

'Oh, Cap'n,' said the voice. 'Ye gave us a start, ye did.'

'Captain?' said Thaddeus. He looked around, expecting to see Pepperjack. But there was no one there.

He turned back to the voice. It belonged to a see-through man. *A ghost*, thought Thaddeus, correcting himself.

'So we're dead then,' he said desolately. He wondered if the ship was some sort of ghost ship. It certainly looked it with all the candles flickering along the rails and deck against the black night.

'Ye ain't be dead, Cap'n, just a bit drowned.' The ghost jiggled his leg, trying to shake off spots of water from his ragged knee breeches.

'Why do you keep calling me Captain?' Thaddeus was very confused. He wondered if partially drowned victims behaved in the same way as people who'd got lost in a desert without any water. Maybe this was all some sort of mirage?

''Cause you be Cap'n of the *Sea Cat*. You do

be the Cap'n, ain't ye?' said the ghost, still eyeing the box covetously.

'I don't understand, how did we get on this ship?' asked Thaddeus. His mind was still whirling and seemed unable to catch hold of any sensible thought.

'Tell 'ims, Billy,' said the ghost, and another ghost man moved into Thaddeus's vision.

The two were identical. Maybe the water *had* addled his brain.

'Billy be my brother,' said the first ghost, setting Thaddeus's mind briefly at ease. So they were twins.

'Tell 'ims, Billy,' the first ghost said again, still staring longingly at the box.

'Alrights then,' Billy said grumpily, clearly annoyed at his brother's loose tongue. 'Ye uncorked the bottle. We's been in there for hundreds of years – quite happy, mind – and then ye uncorked it and the ship swelled and scooped ye all up on her deck.'

'But look, Billy, look – now we sees the stars,' his brother said, glancing away from the box and up at the night sky. 'We never seen the stars, not in forever. We just be lyin' wrecked at the bottom of Davy Jones's Locker. But now we sees the stars.' He clasped his hands together, like a child in prayer.

Thaddeus suddenly became more aware of his surroundings. There were indeed stars in the sky, and a crescent moon, and all around them an ocean softly slapping against the hull of a ship. Somehow they had escaped the *Black Wyddah* and were now sailing on the *Sea Cat*, the tiny ship that had been contained in the bottle the Sea Witch gave him. *His* ship.

The thought of the *Wyddah* brought Thaddeus unsteadily to his feet so he could scan the darkness around him.

'She be long gone, that ways,' said Billy, pointing in the opposite direction to which the *Sea Cat* was travelling.

'Long gone,' echoed the first ghost.

'Back to the nest, Pip,' said Billy, pointing his brother to the foremast.

He turned to Thaddeus and tapped his head discreetly. 'He be doin' no harm, just tooken one too many tumbles from the nest. He's what killed us – he fell and landed on top of me, brokes both our necks. On that very spot, where that whale-boy be sleepin'.'

Billy directed Thaddeus's gaze to a mound lying limply against the mainmast. Thaddeus could easily have taken it for a water barrel.

He hurried over and nudged his friend. 'Juniper, wake up.'

Juniper moved slightly but kept on snoring. After two near drownings in one night, Thaddeus thought he probably wouldn't be waking up anytime soon.

'What about my other friend, Molly?' Thaddeus asked Billy. His memory was returning and he last remembered seeing Molly being pulled down into the ocean's depths by her tail.

Billy looked puzzled. 'No girl, Cap'n, justs a big fish. It be a good catch. Will you be wantin' it for yer dinner, Cap'n?'

Thaddeus laughed. 'No, thanks, Billy, I'm not in the habit of eating my friends. And you'd better not let Molly hear you say that. She has tail issues, and an invisible knife she likes to use occasionally. Where is she anyway?'

Billy's face had taken on a decidedly yellow hue. 'I didn't know, Cap'n, I swears it. I didn't know she be yer friend.'

'Where's Molly, Billy. What have you done to her?' Thaddeus's tone was sharp. He'd never forgive himself if Billy had already cooked Molly for dinner.

Billy pointed upwards and Thaddeus's eyes followed. They almost toppled right out of their sockets at what he saw.

Molly was trussed up in a net and hanging upside down from the yardarm, with a gag in her mouth to silence the abuse that had no doubt been frothing forth at her captors. Thaddeus didn't know how the twins could have got her up there, but there she was, swaying in the wind like a caterpillar in a chrysalis.

Billy suddenly realised that Molly now had legs where her tail had been. 'I swears it, Cap'n, she be havin' no legs when we tied her up. A great big fish she was.'

He dragged his fingers through his tangled hair in worried puzzlement. Thaddeus was finding it very hard to suppress the laughter that was gurgling in his throat. He knew he mustn't let it out. Molly would never speak to him again.

'Untie her at once,' he said, his voice a bubbling squeak rather than the authoritative tone he'd been going for.

Nevertheless, Billy leapt to do his bidding, yelling for Pip to come help. Together they scrambled up the mainmast with the agility of monkeys climbing a coconut tree and lowered Molly softly to the deck.

Thaddeus, his laughter under control, bent and untied the gag.

'LET ME AT THEM!' roared Molly, struggling wildly within her cocoon.

Thaddeus looked up. Billy and Pip were gazing down through the sails with wide eyes.

'We's not be comin' down just yet, Cap'n,' Billy said, and both ghosts disappeared behind the sails.

Now the silent night was broken only by Molly's furious muttering as she tried to break free of the net.

'Would you get me out of here?' she stormed at Thaddeus.

He awkwardly unrolled her from the net, and had to steady her as she stumbled to her feet. Still giddy, she most likely would have staggered overboard without his help. The moment she got her bearings, she raced to the mainmast and attempted to scale it.

'It's harder than it looks,' she mumbled angrily and had to content herself with waving her fist towards where Billy and Pip where hiding. 'You manky ghosts! Just wait until I get a hold of you. Ghosts or no ghosts, you'll be feeling the point of my knife in your bellies!'

'Cap'n, oh, Cap'n, makes her go away,' pleaded Pip.

'Listen here, you no good wisps of nothing –'

'Molly, it was an honest mistake,' interrupted Thaddeus reasonably.

'Oh, alright then.' Molly's voice became persuasive. 'Come down here, little ghosts. I've got something for you if you do. How about a peek in the box there? You liked the box, didn't you? If you come down, it's all yours.'

'MOLLY!' Thaddeus warned.

'She be a tricksy one, Cap'n. We's not be comin' downs till she be gone.'

With that, Billy and Pip refused to acknowledge Thaddeus and Molly any further.

Molly let loose a torrent of abuse. It didn't make any difference. Billy and Pip stayed put and silent.

'Aw, come on, Molly, they didn't mean it,' said Thaddeus. The brothers were beginning to grow on him. Of course, it had nothing to do with the way they called him Captain.

Molly left the mast and came over to where Thaddeus was trying to rouse Juniper. 'Here,' she said, handing him the cork from the bottle. She must have held onto it the entire time she was nearly drowning. 'I see you didn't drop the box,' she added.

Thaddeus had picked it up again the moment he'd freed Molly from the net and was now holding it protectively to his chest. It seemed Molly was immune to its charms and he wondered if it was because she was a sea nymph.

'I think I'd die first rather than lose it,' he said honestly, even though he could still see a red weal slashed across his palm. He rubbed the worn metal of the box. It felt like a shell that had being smoothed for years by the sea.

'What do you suppose is really in here?' he asked Molly. 'I mean, to me it feels like all the power in the world – well, enough to reverse every bad thing that's happened in my life. But to Juniper it just smells like really, really good food. Then there's those two.' He flicked his gaze towards the two figures still sitting sullenly on the yardarm. 'I overheard them saying it has life inside it. But it's not big enough to hold all those things.'

Molly shrugged uncertainly. 'Maybe it doesn't contain any of them. Maybe it's just a ruse to get you to open it. You know – it plays on the deepest desire of the person closest to it so they're desperate to open it. It's a box full of things felt but not seen.'

Thaddeus thought about this. Put that way, it made sense. It probably was just a trick and he'd be well rid of the stupid box. He'd happily bury it in some stinking grave.

'Molly, the Unknown Grave … did the Sea Witch say why we had to bury it there?' He felt heat rush into his cheeks. 'I wasn't exactly listening, you know … when she was talking …'

Molly rolled her eyes. 'No, I don't suppose you were. She only said that the Unknown Grave is a place where you can bury things and the sea comes and swallows them. No one can ever get the items back – they become lost forever, unknown. I guess that's how it got its name.'

'Cap'n, do she be calm yet?'

The wind had picked up and the sails were beginning to buck worse than a wild pony. Billy's tone said he didn't like it much.

Thaddeus laughed and looked at Molly.

She smiled weakly and shrugged. 'What could I do to hurt a ghost anyway?'

'We could be showin' you round yer ship, Cap'n. We knows it for hundreds of years.'

Billy's voice had a pleading note and Thaddeus couldn't leave them hanging up there any longer.

'All hands on deck,' he called.

The twins wafted down and paused at the bottom of the mast, eyeing Molly warily. She turned her back to them and focused on Juniper, who was waking.

'I say, are we dead?' he asked blearily, looking

past Molly to the ghostly twins.

'Not dead, just on a ship out of a bottle,' said Thaddeus. 'We're finally away from those stinking pirates and we have our own ship.' His heart beat gleefully as he brought Juniper up to date. 'And this is Billy and his brother Pip,' he finished.

The twins nodded a hello, but didn't dare shake Juniper's extended hand because that would have brought them closer to Molly.

'We be takin' ye round the *Sea Cat* now, Cap'n,' Billy said, and floated off with Pip close behind. 'That be the mainsail, Cap'n, with the foremast at the front, and the mizzenmasts backs 'ere.'

He went into great detail about the different sails until Thaddeus found himself yawning.

'Show 'ims the Cap'n's cabin, Billy, show 'ims,' said Pip.

Billy wafted to the stern and straight through the bulkhead door. Thaddeus opened the door and followed the ghost into the Captain's quarters. It was a spacious room, well lit by flickering lanterns. In the centre of the room was a wooden table littered with parchments, weathered maps and charts all covered with globs of wax from the swaying iron candelabra above. A spyglass rolled gently to and fro on the table with the movement of the *Sea Cat*.

Thaddeus's eyes moved to the side wall, where two doors beckoned.

'That be yer sleepin' quarters, Cap'n,' said Billy.

Thaddeus opened the first door and a smile formed on his lips. The room was rectangular in shape, with two tall beds built into the side walls, each surrounded by heavy velvet drapes. The mattresses were plump and looked like they were stuffed with the finest duck down. Thaddeus resisted the urge to bounce on one.

'I say, old chap, beats a hammock any day,' said Juniper, walking over to one of the beds and prodding it with his finger. 'Which one shall I take then?'

Thaddeus was glad that Juniper had assumed they'd be sharing the room. It meant that Juniper wasn't with him only because they'd been thrust together by circumstance. Juniper thought of him as a friend.

Now they needed to find a place for Molly to sleep. He stepped out of the room and opened the other door. This cabin was furnished the same as the first, except for the accessories on the bedside table that showed it had once held a female occupant.

He looked at Molly. 'What do you think?'

She smiled with pleasure, especially when Pip said, 'We ain't be goin' in there. She wouldn't be likin' it.'

He and Billy hovered at the doorway, not daring to cross the threshold.

'She?' asked Thaddeus. He was remembering the last time he'd heard the word used in a similar way – by Skip in reference to the Sea Witch.

'The Sad Lady,' Billy said. He drifted back into the main cabin and pointed to the starboard wall. It held a floor-to-ceiling bookcase filled with books of all different shapes and sizes. They were displayed facing outwards, like picture frames, and each cover showed a different person. Billy was pointing to one with a portrait of a woman wearing a veil over her face. 'Hers be the only memoir we can't be openin'. The reason for her sadness be a secret.'

Thaddeus stared at the Sad Lady's face behind its veil. He felt she was oddly familiar, but couldn't see enough of her features to know why. He picked up the heavy volume and tried to open it, but it remained firmly fastened. He replaced it neatly on the shelf.

'Sometimes we be seein' the Sad Lady roamin' about,' Billy continued. 'Her and Bones do be appearin' when the *Sea Cat* be in trouble.'

'Bones?' asked Thaddeus. He was wondering how many ghosts lived aboard the *Sea Cat*.

'Bones do be the skeleton fiddler. But he only be playin' his tunes when the ship be in danger of sinkin',' said Pip, who was running his hands lovingly over the other memoirs on the shelves. 'Tell the Cap'n, Billy, tell 'ims. The memoirs, they all be tellin' us good stories.'

He picked up a book whose cover showed a pirate deserted on an island. A monkey was running up the trunk of a coconut tree, the pirate's stolen tricorn hat looped in its tail.

'That be Nathaniel Barfellow's memoir,' said Billy, taking the volume out of Pip's hand and replacing it on its shelf.

Juniper's stomach let out a low rumble, like distant thunder.

'I say, I don't suppose there's something to nibble on while we tour the rest of the ship?' he asked the twins. 'Food has been rather scarce of late.'

'We be goin' to the galley next,' Billy said, sinking through the floor and beckoning Thaddeus to follow. A few seconds later his sheepish face reappeared. 'I keeps forgettin', Cap'n. We be needin' to take the long way.'

As Thaddeus headed for the door, he

remembered the box in his arms. 'Billy, is there anywhere safe I can leave this?'

The mention of the box brought desire flooding back into the faces of Juniper and the twins.

'It be safe on your desk here, Cap'n,' Billy said, but his eyes looked shifty.

Juniper licked his lips. 'Billy's right, old chap, no one will come after it in here.'

Molly glared at them all. 'Oh, like we're just going to take your word for it!'

'Tell 'ims 'bout the Cap'n's sand, Billy, tell 'ims,' Pip piped up.

'Shhh!' Billy glared murderously at his twin.

'Billy, as your Captain I order you to tell me about the sand,' Thaddeus said with as much authority as he could muster.

Billy wafted about a bit, seeming unsure whether or not to obey Thaddeus's order. Finally, he said grudgingly, 'Alrights then,' and drifted over to the window seat. He flipped the lid open and pointed inside to a glass-like cylinder.

Thaddeus leaned in and took out the cylinder. It was filled with sand. He placed it in the centre of the desk and waited for an explanation.

'What are you waiting for, Wafty? Tell him!' Molly tried to prod Billy in the back but her hand went right through him.

Billy folded his arms huffily across his chest. 'It be the Cap'n's safe. The Cap'n be the only one who can put things in the sand and take things out.'

Thaddeus lifted the box and placed it gently on top of the cylinder. Even though the box was bigger than the cylinder's opening, it sank easily through the glass and was gobbled up by the sand within.

'I say, it's like quicksand,' Juniper said, then he walked briskly to the door, his stomach grumbling loudly. 'To the galley, chaps!'

Thaddeus wasn't quite ready to leave the box yet. He didn't know Billy well enough to trust him, and he still didn't like the overly bright shine in Juniper's eyes, nor the fact that he seemed awfully eager to get them all out of the room. He suspected that Juniper was planning on sneaking back later alone. And Billy and Pip could drift in and out anytime they wanted. Thaddeus wanted proof that he alone was able to access the box.

'Pip, catch!' he said, and threw the cylinder at the ghost lingering by the door.

Pip caught it instinctively and was immediately swallowed by the sand. Thaddeus smiled and picked the cylinder up off the floor. He reached in until he felt something grab his hand. He pulled – and Pip emerged, covered in sand. He stood there unhappily, dripping sand all over the cabin floor.

Thaddeus was satisfied. He left the cylinder on the table, rolling around gently with the spyglass, and moved to the cabin door.

'I say, was that really necessary, old chap?'

Juniper made it sound like he was scolding Thaddeus for tricking Pip into the cylinder. Thaddeus knew better.

'To the galley, Billy,' he said, echoing Juniper's earlier words.

Billy took one last longing look at the cylinder before wafting out of the cabin. He was clearly miffed, because he gave the rest of the tour in a stilted voice. There were four levels to the *Sea Cat*. On the top deck, the same deck as the Captain's cabin, were the ship's cannons, which were not to be left loaded due to the twins' allergies. An off-chance sneeze from either of them could prove disastrous. Cannons were such touchy things.

Also on the top deck were the ratlines – thin ropes tied between the sails that the crew could use to climb up the sails when necessary. Pip informed Thaddeus that the ratlines were prone to sulking, and it wasn't worth going up them if they weren't in a good mood as they had a bad habit of bungeeing you far out to sea.

Pip also confided to Thaddeus that the top deck had an opening to a secret passageway, but it seemed Billy was in no mood to divulge any further information about it.

The second deck held more sleeping cabins, some storage space and the galley. Here, Juniper stopped and refused to go any further.

'But there still be more to shows ye, ain't there, Billy? Tell 'ims.' Pip was somersaulting in the air above their heads, his experience within the Captain's safe clearly forgotten.

Billy nodded. 'Aye, much more. There be the armoury, and the bilge, and –'

'And the poop deck,' interjected Pip.

'I say, I don't like the sound of that,' said Juniper.

'It be the place where the pigeons lives,' Billy explained. 'We uses 'ems as messengers. But I be warnin' ye, Cap'n, ye must always be lockin' the door to the poop deck. Thomas – he be the ship's cat – he be likin' a tasty pigeon for 'ims dinner.' He glanced at Molly warily and added, 'He also be likin' fish.'

Thaddeus couldn't believe the ship was really his. He was so absorbed by all the twins were telling him that he didn't notice Juniper's panicked glances around the galley.

'I say, where's the cook?' asked Juniper. 'Where's the oven for that matter?'

Thaddeus looked around too, and saw that the galley was as un-kitchen-like as a room could be. The only thing it contained was a giant table in its centre, surrounded by chairs, and a potbelly stove in one corner, which he assumed would be lit for warmth during the colder months at sea.

'There ain't no need for a cook or a stove on the *Sea Cat*,' said Billy, pulling out a chair and sitting down.

Thaddeus, Molly, Juniper and Pip followed his lead.

'You just be imaginin' what you wants.'

A leg of lamb swimming in gravy appeared on a large plate before Billy, with a jar of rum next to it.

Juniper was speechless. He blinked and a wide smile stretched his lips. Suddenly the table was laden with a whole buffet of dishes. There was a platter piled high with roast beef, roast potatoes and steaming vegetables. Alongside it stood a mountain of Yorkshire puddings dripping with gravy and whole basket of French fries. Juniper had barely dug in when a pavlova, three different colours of jelly and a whopping chocolate cake appeared.

Thaddeus imagined himself some Mexican tacos with lashings of sour cream and cheese. It was his favourite meal and one that he always helped his mum prepare. But when it appeared, he felt a lump form in his throat and he changed his mind and helped himself to some of Juniper's food instead.

Molly was busy shoving chocolate pudding with dollops of vanilla ice cream into her mouth as if she had never tasted food before.

Miaowing beneath the table heralded the arrival of Thomas the ship's cat. He was a fat black cat with a white stripe on his chest, and he wound himself in and out of Thaddeus's legs until a bowl of sardines was imagined and placed on the floor.

'Did you have to give him fish?' asked Molly, irritated.

Thaddeus shrugged. 'He's got to eat.'

'Agreed,' said Juniper, 'although by the looks of him he's not been starved – unlike us, hey, Thaddeus? The food on the *Wyddah* was terrible in comparison to this!' A glass of something dark and fizzy appeared next to his hand. He picked it up and took a giant gulp, followed quickly by a loud burp. 'I say, I wonder where the *Wyddah* is now. Do you think they've discovered the sea chest is empty yet?'

'You have something on your face,' Molly told him, and pointed to a trickle of gravy slowly making its way from the corner of Juniper's mouth to his chin.

'I say, thanks, Molly.' Juniper dug around in his pocket for something to wipe away the gravy. He pulled out a handful of squashed biscuits, an old sweet wrapper, a sandy shell, and the Buccaneers Chart the Sea Witch had given him. But no handkerchief. He delved his hand into his other pocket.

'Ye could just imagines a napkin,' suggested Billy.

Juniper beamed. A clean white napkin landed in his palm.

'Juniper! The chart!' Thaddeus said.

His tone silenced the clatter of cutlery. Everyone stared at the folded parchment. It was no longer blank.

CHAPTER THIRTEEN

THE BUCCANEERS CHART

'Unfold it,' said Molly.

She pushed her pudding away from her and it immediately disappeared. She moved to pick up the parchment, but Thaddeus got there first. They watched intently as an inked miniature hand holding a quill squiggled speedily over the parchment.

'It's a map!' Thaddeus exclaimed excitedly, unfolding it and placing it in the middle of the table.

What had been a blank page before was now smothered with squiggles that represented the ocean. In the middle was the *Sea Cat*, travelling under full sail. Some distance behind it was another ship, currently in the process of making a wide turn.

Pip was the first to speak. 'It be the *Wyddah*,

Billy, the *Black Wyddah*!' he squeaked.

'He's right,' said Molly with a frown. 'They must have realised we're gone and they're coming after us.'

Thaddeus jumped up. If they got caught before he'd made good on his bargain with the Sea Witch, they'd be back to square one.

'We have to find the Unknown Grave and we have to find it now,' he said. 'Billy, do you know of any charts that show such a place?'

Billy scratched his head thoughtfully. 'We's never be hearin' of the Unknown Grave, Cap'n.'

Thaddeus looked at Juniper's chart. The *Wyddah* had completed her turn and was after them. He imagined they had four hours' head-start, but no more. And the *Wyddah* had a full crew that would be working hard to shorten the distance. The *Sea Cat* had a crew of five, all of whom were still sitting in the galley. And three of them had no idea how to sail a ship!

He pulled Juniper's chair out and the buffet of dishes disappeared.

'I say, old chap, I wasn't done yet.' Juniper made to tuck his chair back in and reimagine his food.

'Oh no, you don't, Jupe. We need to find the Unknown Grave, and the only way we're going to do that is if you can bring it up on this chart of yours. The same way you just did with the *Sea Cat* and the *Wyddah*.'

'But I don't know how I did that,' protested Juniper.

'Just think about the Unknown Grave,' said Molly. 'Imagine it in your mind.'

'I can't!' he spluttered. 'How can I imagine a place that I've never seen before?'

'It seems to me you can easily imagine the things you want to – like that buffet you just produced!' snapped Molly. Turning to Thaddeus, she added, 'I think it's just an excuse. We all know he's still upset that you won't let him hold the box.'

'I say!' Juniper's face had become very red and frown lines wrinkled across his forehead. 'That's not the case at all, Molly! You have the wrong end of the stick – as usual. You'll see.'

With that he stared at the map with intense concentration. It shimmered at first, then faded to blank again, and then the hand and the quill reappeared to draw different markings. The *Sea Cat* was still on the ocean, but now bits of land appeared as well, forming an island that was marked with a big red X.

Molly smirked. Thaddeus began to feel hopeful.

'Keep thinking, Jupe. Think about how we get there,' he encouraged.

Juniper closed his eyes and breathed heavily. The hand drew a dotted line across the parchment – a path for the *Sea Cat* to follow. Thaddeus cheered, only to be checked by Molly.

'We're going the wrong way!' she said.

Thaddeus looked more closely at the chart. Molly was right. They needed to head west.

'All hands on deck,' he ordered. 'Billy, we need your help to teach us how to sail the *Sea Cat*. It's going to be a long night!'

***

All through the night, Thaddeus, Molly and Juniper laboured with the *Sea Cat*'s sails under Billy's tutelage and with the occasional comment from Pip. It was hard work and by the time the first rays of dawn washed over the ocean, all three children were exhausted.

'You'd think a magical ship like the *Sea Cat* would be able to sail itself,' moaned Juniper, flopping onto the deck for a rest.

'Land ho!' yelled Pip from up in the nest.

Thaddeus looked at the Buccaneers Chart. The *Sea Cat* was almost at the island where the

Unknown Grave was located.

'Good job,' he told everyone.

'I say, old chap, can't we anchor and rest a while?' Juniper asked. 'I'm awfully tired and it's way past breakfast time.'

Thaddeus ignored him and consulted the chart again. He wanted to see how far the *Wyddah* was behind them. It had covered more distance in the long night than the *Sea Cat* had – so much so that Thaddeus turned to look behind him, expecting to see the *Wyddah*'s mast and white sails. The horizon was empty, however, save for a scattering of puffy clouds. He looked back at the chart. It wouldn't be long now until they reached their destination. They just needed to round the cape of the island, and then anchor the *Sea Cat* in a small inlet near to where the Unknown Grave was marked.

'Molly, you and Jupe have breakfast,' he said. 'I'll stay and guide the ship around the cape – but make sure he's quick.'

By the time Molly and Juniper returned, the sun was well up in the sky and Thaddeus had rounded the cape and was following the line of sun-washed white cliffs into the inlet, being careful to stay in line with the chart's direction. It wouldn't do to stray, because a dangerous reef was marked on the chart to the starboard of the *Sea Cat*.

'Should be furlin' the sails now, Cap'n,' Billy said, his gaze fixed dreamily on the fluffy clouds above.

'Furl the sails,' yelled Thaddeus, handing Juniper the Buccaneers Chart.

Molly and Juniper stared at him. Neither of them moved.

'Come on, get to work, you two. Billy says we should be furling the sails.'

'And furl them we will, just as soon as we know how,' Molly said, crossing her arms over her chest and glaring at Billy. 'And why isn't he helping? He and Pip have done none of the work themselves. They just tell us what to do before wafting away.'

Billy continued to stare at the clouds. 'What d'ye s'pose them clouds tastes like, Cap'n? Pip says one slapped 'im in the face once when he be up in the nest. He says it be tastin' like milk. I ain't believin' him though 'cause he ain't got a white moustache to prove it.'

Thaddeus looked at the ghost in disbelief. Didn't he know how urgent matters were? The box was still unburied, and the *Wyddah* was hot on their tail, and all Billy could think about was what flavour the clouds might be. The twins were no help at all! He suspected that if their young lives hadn't been cut short by Pip's accident, the *Sea Cat*'s original Captain might have found a different way to get rid of them.

'Billy, you need to help Molly and Juniper furl the sails,' said Thaddeus impatiently.

'Alrights then,' said Billy grudgingly. He wafted to a standing position and did his best to stomp towards the mizzenmast, but without effect as it was impossible for a ghost to stomp. He shouted instructions instead.

By the time the *Sea Cat*'s sails were all furled and her anchor dropped, Molly and Juniper were glaring hatefully at the bossy ghost.

'I be goin' now, Cap'n,' said Billy, wafting up to the safety of the nest.

'How do we get from the ship to the beach, old chap?' Juniper asked Thaddeus as he slumped in exhaustion against the mast. Before Thaddeus could answer, Juniper had closed his tired eyes and within seconds was snoring worse than a pair of pigs in a pigpen.

'That's the easy part,' said Thaddeus, squinting at the sandy beach. 'We take the longboat. I'm more concerned about the *Sea Cat*. The Witch told me to keep her on me always.'

'I would think that you just take the cork out of the bottle and she'll find her way back inside,' said Molly, moving to the rail and looking dismally at the small longboat attached to the ship's side. 'If that's the case, we should probably just sail right onto the beach and then uncork the bottle. That seems safer.'

'The fish girl be wantin' to beach us, Billy!' Pip cried. 'That ain't good. Tell the Cap'n, Billy, tell 'ims.'

Thaddeus had been thinking Molly's idea wasn't half-bad. He looked enquiringly up at Billy, who was watching guardedly from the nest.

'Pip be right, Cap'n,' Billy said. 'Ye must never be beachin' the *Sea Cat*. She can only get in and out of her bottle if she be in the sea.' His voice took on a hopeful tone. 'Will ye be takin' the box with ye, Cap'n? It be safe here on the *Sea Cat* in the Cap'n's sand. You knows no one can get onto the ship without yer permission. The rails be turnin' to liquid, see – nothin' for a grapplin' hook to be grabbin' onto. Ye could just keep the box here, Cap'n.'

Thaddeus seriously considered it, until a burning sensation in his hand brought him back to his senses. 'Not a good idea, Billy.'

'I's just be suggestin' it, Cap'n,' said Billy

dejectedly.

Molly moved closer to Thaddeus. He could tell she was still feeling sour towards the twins, particularly Billy.

'I don't think you can trust him,' she warned.

'Let's not forget who the Captain is here,' said Thaddeus, stomping towards his cabin and feeling annoyed at Molly's authoritative tone. *Girls, who needs them?* he thought.

He picked up the cylinder of sand and held it for a moment. If only he hadn't made that bargain with the Sea Witch. She was so slippery. He plunged his hand into the glass cylinder and felt around the sand inside. His fingers closed around the box and he withdrew it, then made his way back to the deck where Molly was waiting.

'Got everything you need, *Captain*? Would you like me to help with anything, *Captain*? Your word is my command, *Captain*!'

Her tone was sarcastic and her stare withering. Thaddeus didn't have time for it.

'Look here, Molly,' he began, then paused, his eyes going past her face to the horizon. Was that a sail, or just another fluffy white cloud?

Molly spun around, forgetting her crabbiness. 'What is it?'

'I don't know … it could be the *Wyddah*'s sail

… but could they be that close so soon? I can't decide … is it a sail or a cloud? If it's a sail, it might not be safe to go to the Unknown Grave.'

Molly whipped out the spyglass the Sea Witch had given her and scoured the horizon in the direction Thaddeus was looking. Almost immediately, she fell over backwards.

'It's the *Wyddah* and they're awfully close,' she gasped. 'They're almost on top of us – we're going to have to make a run for it!'

Her panic woke Juniper, who sat up with a start.

Thaddeus stared at Molly. What was she on about? He couldn't see anything close enough to make her react as she had. He wasn't even sure what he'd seen was a sail. It could just be a cloud.

'I say, Molly, maybe you have a touch of sunstroke,' Juniper said helpfully. 'Perhaps you should take a nap in your cabin.'

He staggered to his feet, but stopped when he realised Thaddeus was holding the box again. His eyes fixated on it and Thaddeus saw his tiredness evaporate.

'Well, you'll be sorry when they crash right into us, won't you!' Molly snapped.

Thaddeus took the spyglass from her and looked through it himself. All he saw was a kaleidoscope of shattered glass. Not that it meant anything. Juniper's Buccaneers Chart had been blank, and Thaddeus was standing on the deck of a ship that had been handed to him in a bottle.

He passed Caspian's Eye back to Molly. The Sea Witch had said it would show her everything she needed to know. That meant if Molly said the *Wyddah* was close, then the *Wyddah* *was* close.

'Tell me exactly what you see,' he said to her.

Molly replaced the spyglass against her eye. 'The *Wyddah*. She's raised her flag, but it's red, not black –'

She stopped and shuddered, an expression of horror filling her face. Pip had toppled from the nest, landed smack on top of her and fallen straight through her. Thaddeus tried not to laugh.

'Why you slimy, cold…! Don't you ever touch me again,' said Molly.

Pip quickly floated out of her way, wringing his pale hands. 'Did the fish girl say a red flag? Oh, Cap'n, the *Wyddah* be raisin' the No Mercy flag. We all be goin' to die!' He looked up to where Billy was leaning out of the nest. 'We be goin' to die, Billy, again.'

'They're absolutely bonkers,' said Juniper, edging closer to Thaddeus.

Thaddeus agreed. Especially considering Pip

was now combing the deck for a hiding spot.

'Calls the Sad Lady, Billy, calls her,' he shouted up to his twin. 'And Bones. We be needin' the fiddler to play us to our deaths. Call 'ems, Billy, call 'ems.'

Thaddeus closed his ears to Pip's plaintive wails. 'How far away are they?' he asked Molly tersely.

'I don't know. Through the spyglass it looks like I could almost touch their sails.' She reached out her hand and waved it gently as if stroking something.

Thaddeus turned to Juniper. 'What does the chart say? Can it show us time as well as distance?'

Juniper rustled around in his pocket and brought out the Buccaneers Chart. 'Here, I'll hold the box while you look at it,' he told Thaddeus, licking his lips and swallowing.

'Not likely,' said Thaddeus.

He held onto the box tightly with one hand and grabbed the chart with the other, shaking out its folds and laying it on the deck. They all three stared at it.

'Think about how far away the *Wyddah* is in time,' Thaddeus urged.

Juniper screwed up his face and focused intently on the chart. The ocean faded, as did the anchored *Sea Cat* and the still sailing *Wyddah*. The parchment rippled and the small hand and quill drew a new image – Juniper holding the box with a satisfied smile on his face. Before Thaddeus could comment, the drawing disappeared and was quickly replaced by two hourglasses.

'Two hours. That's what it means, right?' asked Thaddeus.

Molly nodded, but she was looking at Juniper worriedly. 'I think we should just go now, before it's too late.'

Thaddeus caught her meaning and clutched the box more firmly.

Juniper didn't notice anything. 'I say, that's a great idea. We don't want Silver getting his hands on the box. Let's go.' And he hurried to the side of the ship where the longboat was fastened.

Molly refolded the chart and slipped it into her pocket. She hesitated at the rail, clearly not eager to get any water on her skin, but another glance at Juniper's glazed eyes decided her. She climbed over the side and sat herself firmly in the middle of the longboat.

Thaddeus climbed in after her. It wasn't that easy with only one hand free. Juniper offered to take the box for him to make it easier.

'Do you think I'm that stupid?' Thaddeus said

curtly.

Juniper scowled and slumped heavily onto his seat, causing the longboat to rock wildly against the side of the *Sea Cat*.

Thaddeus placed the box tightly between his knees, and he and Molly quickly lowered the ropes that held the longboat in place. When they were bobbing around on the water, Thaddeus reached for the bottle hanging on its cord around his neck.

'Let's hope this works,' he said, and pulled the cork.

The *Sea Cat* rocked for a second, then disappeared with a sound like someone sucking milkshake through a straw. Thaddeus looked at the bottle in his hand. The ship was now safely inside. He replaced the cork.

'Two hours,' reminded Molly.

They each picked up a set of oars and rowed awkwardly to the shore. Molly refused to get out of the boat until Thaddeus and Juniper had pulled it high onto the beach. It took a lot of effort and they were sweating profusely by the time she allowed her feet to touch the dry white sand.

'Where to now?' asked Thaddeus, enjoying the feel of warm sand beneath his toes despite his worry.

Juniper tore his eyes from the box when he

realised Thaddeus was talking to him. 'I ... uh ... I'm sorry, old chap, I think I left the Buccaneers Chart on the *Sea Cat.*'

He looked sheepish, until Molly drew the parchment out of her pocket and handed it to him.

'You should take more care of the Sea Witch's gift,' she lectured.

Juniper took the chart without a word and unfolded it. He closed his eyes and Thaddeus knew he was trying his best to focus on asking the chart where the Unknown Grave was. He and Molly leaned in and watched the chart as it transformed yet again. Now they were on dry land, it seemed the chart had become a tracking device. Three miniatures of Thaddeus, Molly and Juniper appeared on the map in the very spot they were standing on, then a set of footprints directed them three hundred paces along the beach.

Thaddeus started walking and counting. Juniper followed, sticking so close to Thaddeus and the box that his elbows soon became a problem.

'Two hundred and ninety-nine,' said Thaddeus through gritted teeth, annoyed by Juniper's proximity. 'Three hundred.'

They had reached a sandbank that ran parallel to the ocean along the stretch of beach, presumably carved out by the high tides.

Juniper consulted the chart. 'It's telling us to climb over this sandbank and go through the trees. We should come to another beach.'

He shoved the Buccaneers Chart under his arm and struggled to heave himself over the bank. All three children pushed through the jungle-like trees to find themselves on the edge of an isolated beach the shape of a crescent moon. High cliffs protected it each side, except for the small gap they'd come through. Offshore was a long stretch of reef with waves crashing onto it.

Thaddeus hesitated before stepping onto the sand. 'Is this the only way in and out?' he asked.

Juniper consulted the map. 'There's a thin line straight through the middle of the reef, but I wouldn't like to try sailing through it. Look at what the hand is drawing.'

Thaddeus and Molly stared at the map. It showed the surging waves smashing over the top of reef, with a graveyard of ships beneath the water.

Footprints reappeared, directing them to one end of the crescent beach beneath an overhanging cliff. It was marked with a large black cross.

'X marks the spot,' said Thaddeus. 'Where's the *Wyddah*, Molly?'

Molly raised Caspian's Eye and peered into the jungle behind them. 'Still sailing around the cape of the island.'

'We'd better hurry,' said Thaddeus and he took off down the beach, following the footprints dotted along the map.

The sun was hot and they were all sweating by the time they reached the spot. It didn't help that the box was beginning to weigh on Thaddeus's mind again.

'Doesn't look much. I hope the chart knows what it's doing, ' he said. He could tell from the tide mark on the sand that the Unknown Grave would be completely swallowed by the sea at high tide. 'Hand me the shovel, Molly. Let's get this over with.'

Molly looked at him blankly. 'You didn't tell me to bring a shovel.'

Thaddeus frowned. He looked at Juniper. He was empty-handed too.

'I say, old chap, couldn't we just have a peek inside before we bury it?' Juniper wheedled. 'No one would know.'

Thaddeus groaned inwardly. It was as if the box knew it was about to be disposed of and was sending out one last objection.

'NO!' said Molly loudly. She scanned the beach, but it was pristine save for large clusters of smooth brown rocks here and there. 'If we go back to the trees we should be able to find a big enough stick to use as a shovel. It'll be quicker if you leave the box here, Thaddeus.'

'Are you insane?' he said. He felt his eyes haze over and knew the box wanted to keep him close. 'I'm not leaving it. You two go and I'll wait here with the box.'

'No one gets left behind, remember? That means all three of us go together.'

To her credit, Molly didn't add that Thaddeus clearly couldn't be trusted alone with the box at this particular moment.

'I'll stay with it,' offered Juniper a little too excitedly.

Molly rolled her eyes and gave Thaddeus a sharp poke with her elbow.

'No!' he said. 'Molly's right, Jupe. The box stays and we all go.'

'But what about the pirates?' protested Juniper. 'They could get to it if we leave it unguarded.'

'Nice try,' Molly said, raising her spyglass to her eye. 'The pirates are still at sea. They have to anchor, then row ashore, and even then they'd have to pass us to get to the box. And that's if they even know we have it, which I doubt. The Sea Witch isn't exactly on friendly terms with any of them except for Skip, and I doubt he'd tell the others about the box. They're after us, you know – not the box!'

Thaddeus couldn't think of any more arguments against Molly's common sense. He put the box down, then followed Molly and Juniper back along the beach to the gap. They trudged through the warm sand, Juniper in the lead, his head turning every few seconds to look back at the box.

Thaddeus's own thoughts were still on the box too. He was wondering if Juniper had a point. What if the pirates did get to it first? Maybe he should go back to watch over it. And while he was there, would anyone notice if he opened it? Surely one peek wouldn't do any harm? Then his hand started burning again and he gripped it with his other hand, trying his best to divert his wayward thoughts.

Molly took out Caspian's Eye again and stared through the wall of tropical jungle. She adjusted the lens, then gave a gasp and shoved the spyglass back into her tunic pocket.

'We should hurry,' she told Thaddeus. 'The

Wyddah's anchored in the cove and she's lowering her longboats. Skip's with them. I'd say we have less than an hour now.'

She raced off after Juniper, who had already stumbled into the thicket of trees and was out of sight.

Thaddeus didn't need to be told twice. He hurried after Molly. They needed to bury the box, then get back to the other beach so they could uncork the *Sea Cat* before they were captured. Would they have time? It would take at least fifteen minutes to get the *Sea Cat* under full sail with a crew of three. The twins didn't count. At the slightest hint of manual labour, they wafted up to the nest or disappeared somewhere within the belly of the ship.

Thaddeus reached the trees. He could feel the racing seconds like a heartbeat.

'Where's Jupe?' he asked Molly.

She pointed into the dense foliage. 'I saw him head that way, but that was when I was still on the beach. He could be anywhere by now. I hope he doesn't go too far – he doesn't know the pirates are rowing ashore. What if he runs into them or gets lost?'

Molly was right. Even if Juniper only got lost, it would mean trouble for them all. Too busy thinking to watch where he was putting his feet, Thaddeus tripped over a large thick stick. He kicked it impatiently before realising it would be a perfect digging tool.

'Hey, Molly, we can use this,' he said, bending to pick it up. He noticed half a dozen more just like it. 'And all of these. Look at them, these are perfect ...'

His voice tailed off as his brain asked a persistent question: *Why did Juniper go past these perfectly good digging sticks to go further into the jungle?*

The answer hit him like a bolt of lightning.

He turned and ran back to the gap in the jungle. His eyes landed on Juniper, who was lolloping along the sand like a demented walrus, heading straight for the Sea Witch's box. He must have hidden right by the gap, and once Molly and Thaddeus had passed him he'd returned to the beach.

'JUNIPER!' Thaddeus screamed.

He took a flying leap onto the beach, better than an Olympic pole-vaulter, and tore along the warm sand with Molly hot on his heels.

'JUNIPER ... NOOOO!' yelled Molly.

But Juniper had already reached the box. With shark-like frenzy he tore open the lid.

CHAPTER FOURTEEN

HELLO, PEPPERJACK

It all happened so suddenly. A figure squeezed itself out of the box, like a genie might out of a bottle, and knocked Juniper flying. It stood commandingly on the sand and looked around, a dreadful blot on the vivid landscape.

Thaddeus stopped dead, causing Molly to crash into him. 'What the …?'

His heart plummeted to his feet as he stared at the man who was now smiling at the sun as if he'd been locked away in a dismal place for over a hundred years.

'Who is it?' puffed Molly.

'Pepperjack,' said Thaddeus with certainty. He ducked behind a rock cluster and pulled Molly with him. 'Why didn't we realise? The Sea Witch told us she would only be free if Pepperjack was dead. Then she asked us to bury the box –

aaagggh!' He knocked his fist against his head –
he couldn't believe he'd been so stupid. 'Juniper
and I even watched Pepperjack's memoir – he was
in the cave with the Sea Witch, and she moved her
tail and then it went blank. Don't you see, Molly?
She must have shown Pepperjack the box and it
became the thing he desired the most – *the most
sought-after treasure*! The Sea Witch was bound to
Pepperjack so she couldn't harm him or kill him.
It was his own greed that imprisoned him!'

'Yes!' Molly said. 'And if you'd buried the box
it would have been the end of Pepperjack – but
not by the Sea Witch's doing. So what do we do
now?'

'I'm not sure yet,' said Thaddeus.

He couldn't take his eyes off the figure
strutting around on the sand. Pepperjack was
dressed in black breeches, a white pirate shirt that
laced at the front, and a scarlet overcoat. Atop his
pitch-black hair was the tricorn hat with the red
feathered plume Thaddeus had seen in Timothy
Clegg's memoir; and his jet-black beard came to
a spearhead point on his upper chest. Thick gold
hoops hung from his ears, and tucked into his
waist sash were two pistols and a gleaming sword.

'One thing doesn't make sense,' Molly
whispered. 'Why would the Sea Witch risk us

setting Pepperjack free? Something could have happened – something *has* happened.'

'Yes, but it might not have. Look how close we were to burying the box in the Unknown Grave. The Witch took a chance – a big one. The risk of us opening the box was small in comparison to the freedom she might get from us burying it. Besides, she did her best to make sure we didn't open the box – all that hair-binding promise business.'

Thaddeus rubbed his hand absently. It was aching, reminding him of his still active bargain with the Witch.

Molly noticed. 'Is it painful … will you be able to fight if we need to?'

'It's not as painful as it could be, probably because I wasn't the one to open the box. I should be able to use a weapon – if I had one.'

He looked bitterly at his empty hands. Why hadn't he thought to bring any weapons?

'What should we do?' asked Molly again.

The way she was holding her fist, Thaddeus could tell she had her knife out. Not that it would do much good against the long silver sword that hung from Pepperjack's waist.

'I don't know,' he said slowly. The opening of the box hadn't been planned, and even if it had, Pepperjack was the last thing Thaddeus had expected to find in there. 'Think, think!' He tapped his head in a desperate bid to spur his mind to action.

Pepperjack had finished enjoying the sun and the sea and now turned to face Juniper, who lay frozen with terror on the sand, spittle blubbering from his mouth.

'I should be thanking ye, boy,' said the Captain, nudging Juniper with the toe of a silver-buckled boot.

Juniper wasn't capable of any response other than a wild-eyed look.

Pepperjack slowly removed his sword from its sheath.

'Do something!' gasped Molly.

'So I'll be thanking ye in the best way I know how.' Pepperjack raised his arm high.

Thaddeus leapt out from behind the rock and tore towards Juniper and Pepperjack. 'YOU STINKING FILTHY MAGGOTY PIRATE!' he screamed, hoping to divert Pepperjack's attention.

It worked. Pepperjack turned and a wicked smile broke out on his face.

'RUN, JUNIPER, RUN!' screamed Molly, hot on Thaddeus's heels.

Juniper stumbled to his feet. But there was nowhere to run so he just staggered in a circle.

'Pepperjack will be dealing with ye in a moment!' yelled Pepperjack to Thaddeus and Molly as they charged towards him. And he turned back to Juniper.

Thaddeus was certain that Juniper's life was about to end. His own heart was pounding so hard it felt like it could break through his chest. He couldn't lose his friend, but Juniper was trapped with nowhere to run ... unless ...

'THE BOX!' screamed Thaddeus. 'INTO THE BOX, JUNIPER – HE WON'T FOLLOW YOU THERE.'

Juniper didn't waste any time. As the cutlass swiped at him, he plunged headfirst into the box. It was a spectacular dive for such a hefty form, and had Thaddeus and Molly been judges at a diving contest, they would have awarded him gold for sure.

The cutlass came down a second too late. It sliced the edge of the box, sending sparks onto the white sand. The air rang with a clanging sound.

Thaddeus was right – Pepperjack didn't follow Juniper back into the box. He wasn't keen to revisit his prison. Instead, he kicked the lid shut on Juniper, then turned wrathfully towards

Thaddeus and Molly, rage blowing across his face like a storm at sea. It seemed that a thwarted pirate captain was even more frightening than a vindictive one. He stabbed his sword back into its sheath, pulled two shiny pistols from within the folds of his scarlet jacket and fired.

It was Molly's turn to pull Thaddeus behind a rock. 'He'll shoot you,' she panted as they ducked from the lead balls whizzing over their heads.

'That stinking pirate will have to catch me first. I'm not leaving without Juniper,' thundered Thaddeus.

A hole the size of a large marble appeared in the sand near their feet. Pepperjack was getting closer.

'You'll be no good to Juniper peppered with holes,' warned Molly.

Thaddeus reluctantly gave in to her common sense and they both turned and raced back down the beach, away from the vicious Captain and the box with Juniper trapped inside.

'He's gaining on us,' puffed Molly, chancing a glance over her shoulder.

Suddenly shouts came from the jungle in front of them.

'THERE THEY BE!'

'And there be the Captain!'

'The curse be lifted!'

A group of ragged pirates stumbled onto the sand and ran towards Thaddeus and Molly.

'We're trapped!' panicked Molly.

'Make for the sea,' Thaddeus said, changing direction. 'I'll uncork the *Sea Cat*.'

'But the reef – we won't be able to get her past it. She's too big.'

'We'll have to chance it – we have no choice,' said Thaddeus with forced bravery.

He knew very well that they would need to get past the reef before they could uncork the ship, and he didn't like the look of those galloping white swells thundering against what was hidden below.

He stepped into the water and hesitated. His heart was pounding in his ears and a lump formed in his throat. He took a deep breath and continued wading until he was up to his knees. Then he noticed Molly hadn't followed him.

'Thaddeus … I can't!' she wailed.

He looked back at the beach. The pirates were closing in on them. And Pepperjack was only a stone's throw away on their other side.

'Molly, you can do it!'

Too late. Pepperjack lunged at Molly, knocking her down and into the water. Her legs became useless as they started to transform. The pirate set his black boot on her head, forcing her face into the sea.

The crew reached their Captain and formed a semicircle around him and Molly, laughing and jeering. A couple of them waded into the waves after Thaddeus, but Pepperjack called them back.

'Watch your Captain, ye mongrel dogs. Watch the power that he be wielding.' He mooshed Molly's head deeper into the shallows and crooked a finger at Thaddeus. 'Come back, boy, or your friend dies.'

Thaddeus knew that when Molly transformed she could breathe underwater, so he wasn't worried about her drowning. But he needed to prevent Pepperjack and his crew from realising this. Otherwise, Thaddeus knew without a doubt that Molly would have a sudden appointment with a razor-sharp sword. His job was to keep them talking and distracted.

'If you think you're taking me back to your stinking ship, you can forget it. I'm not going. And what are you doing out of your box anyway, you manky pirate? You should be dead, you no good, thieving rat!'

The pirates were all facing Thaddeus now, which meant Molly was able to complete her transformation behind their backs. But Thaddeus's insults washed over Pepperjack without leaving as much as a drip. Thaddeus felt a sudden icy fear. The Captain wasn't reacting as he'd hoped. At the very least he had expected Pepperjack to leap after him, leaving Molly to swim for safety.

'There be something ye be needing to know,' Pepperjack jeered. 'About Pepperjack's own cleverness.'

Thaddeus snorted, but Pepperjack ignored him.

'Ye see, a man such as Captain Pepperjack, following certain paths, do be making many enemies. Long ago it be made sure that Pepperjack be having the protection of a great wizard. That tricksy Sea Witch, she be thinking to kill Pepperjack. She tried – and failed. She be bound to Pepperjack now and can't be harming him without harming herself. Furious, she be imprisoning Pepperjack in that box – but that meant she be imprisoning herself too. Stupid witch!' Pepperjack laughed heartily. 'The Witch is only being released if she be lifting the lid of the box herself, or Pepperjack be dying. Thanks to your fat friend, neither option be possible for her now.'

The pirates cheered their Captain.

'She wasn't stupid,' Thaddeus said hotly. 'She

knew that if she opened the box herself you'd likely spring out and kill her. So she waited until she could get someone to bury the box for her, and you with it, in a place that would obliterate you forever. Her plan would have worked too if … if …'

'Like Pepperjack said afore – stupid witch! She sent some useless children to do the job for her!' Pepperjack snarled. Suddenly he seemed to realise that Molly hadn't moved in a long while. He released his pressure on her head and called to Thaddeus, 'Your stupid friend be dead. Now it be your turn, boy. Pepperjack be looking forward to wringing your blasted neck.'

The Captain stepped away from Molly and drew his sword. In the same moment, Molly slapped her tail upwards, clobbered the back of his head and sent him flying.

'SERVES YOU RIGHT, YOU STINKING PIRATE!' yelled Thaddeus, aiming a punishing kick at the man now floundering in the waves.

As the pirates blundered into the shallows to help their struggling Captain, Thaddeus pulled Molly deeper into the ocean.

Pepperjack was furious. He leapt up, sword in hand, slashing at the arms of his helpful crew. 'AFTER THEM!' he roared.

The pirates didn't hang about. They dived into the water, their eyes fixed on their prey.

'Hold on, Thaddeus,' said Molly with grim determination.

She gave a flip of her tail and they were off in a zigzag pattern, Thaddeus clinging on tightly and holding his breath as Molly dived beneath each wave.

'Go along the reef until you find the gap,' he called to her. 'We might just get away after all!'

'But what about Juniper?' she protested.

'We just need to deal with these pirates first, then we'll go back for him. Besides, Jupe is safer where he is at the moment.'

Waves thundered over the reef with white foaming fingers that rolled and tumbled the pirates back to the shore and their livid Captain.

Molly swam through the narrow gap in the reef, past the pounding waves, and out to the open sea. Thaddeus grabbed at the bottle around his neck and uncorked the *Sea Cat*. He and Molly were instantly swept up on the swelling ship's deck.

'That was close,' he said, lying on his back and catching his breath.

'Ye be tellin' us, Cap'n,' said Billy. 'We's be makin' bets. We's even called out the fiddler.'

He pointed to a lanky skeleton wearing only a pair of cowboy boots and matching hat with a pistol holstered at his hip. He was loosely holding a violin in his bony hands.

'Thanks for your vote of confidence, Billy,' said Thaddeus wryly.

Billy beamed as if he'd been paid a compliment.

Thaddeus turned back to Molly and grinned. 'You did it, Molly, you did it! Course I always knew you could. Although maybe we need a pool on deck so you can practise how to steer. I thought I was gonna be sick with all that jerking.'

Molly only blushed. It seemed her success had tied her tongue.

Thaddeus leaned over the rail to see what had happened to Captain Pepperjack and the pirates. Pepperjack was standing on the beach, but he wasn't looking at the *Sea Cat*. He was staring past them with such an expression of triumph that Thaddeus got the shivers.

'SHIP AHOY!' shouted Pip, leaning so far out from the nest it was easy to see how he could have plummeted from it to his death.

Thaddeus looked in the direction of Pip's ghostly finger. The *Black Wyddah* had entered the inlet and was closing in fast on the *Sea Cat*. Thaddeus could see figures scurrying to trim the sails, set anchor and lower the longboats to row to the beach to pick up their Captain and the rest of the crew.

'READY THE CANNONS!' Silver roared, his command easily audible aboard the *Sea Cat*.

Billy scampered up the mainmast to the nest, where he and Pip clung to each other like wet kittens.

'You useless stinking …' Words eluded Thaddeus. He shook his fist at the ghosts before helping Molly stand on her jelly legs.

'What should we do?' she asked.

Thaddeus turned back to the *Wyddah*, which was manoeuvring into firing position. He knew that even with Molly's help he wouldn't get the *Sea Cat* under sail in time. Only two options presented themselves.

One was to stand and fight – but he dismissed the idea before it had fully formed. He had no idea how to fire a cannon, and even if he did, the tiny crew of the *Sea Cat* wouldn't stand a chance against the whole battery of cannons aboard the *Wyddah*.

So it really came down to just one other option. He looked at Molly. She wasn't going to like it.

'Not we, *you*,' he said, his words tripping over

each other in their hurry to get out. 'There's only one way out of this – you need to get back in the water and disable the *Wyddah*. I'm thinking if you use your knife, you can cut a hole in her hull so she takes on water and hopefully lists to one side. Noxious doesn't seem to be on deck, which means he's likely still whizzing around upside down in his cabin. Without his help it'll take the pirates ages to fix the hull and give us time to get away.'

Molly shook her head. 'Thaddeus, I can't. I'm tired. This transforming is exhausting, and I haven't slept, and I still can't swim properly …'

Thaddeus tried to sound like a Captain. 'It's the only way, Molly.'

'HARD TO PORT,' screamed Silver. The *Wyddah* was close enough now that Thaddeus could hear the thump, thump, thump of Silver's peg leg as he jumped up and down with anticipatory glee. 'BOOTH! HENRY! GO PICK UP THE CAPTAIN. THE REST OF YE SCURVY DOGS, MAN THE CANNONS! LET'S BE SCUTTLIN' THAT FLEA-RIDDEN CAT!'

A longboat was quickly lowered and began manoeuvring a pathway through the reef. Meanwhile, the *Wyddah* was almost in position to fire her cannons. Silver grinned mercilessly across the water at Thaddeus and the *Sea Cat*.

'Molly … please,' said Thaddeus. His tone was desperate.

Molly didn't answer. She simply dived into the space between the two ships.

Thaddeus anxiously waited on deck. Thomas appeared and weaved around his legs, miaowing.

Billy and Pip began to sing a dirge-like sea shanty and the skeleton fiddler accompanied them.

'Somes say we're bounds for far-off lands,
And aye, that would be grand,
Heave ho, heave ho, away we goes.
But the Cap'n's off his rocker,
So we's bound for Davy Jones's Locker,
Heave ho, heave ho, and downs we gooooo!'

Their singing caused the Sad Lady to appear on the *Sea Cat*'s prow next to Thaddeus. He found her presence oddly encouraging and comforting. The skeleton fiddler raised his violin again and Billy and Pip crooned melodramatically to each other until Thaddeus could stand it no longer.

'SHUT YOUR CORKS!' he yelled, grabbing hold of the nearest thing to hand, which happened to be a clay water jug. He hurled it at the nest with excellent aim and sent Billy plummeting to the deck.

Silence descended with him, and the fiddler scuttled away out of sight. The Sad Lady stayed, her eyes silently taking everything in.

Thaddeus focused his attention back on the *Wyddah*. Her gun ports were open and he could see angry cannon noses jutting out, awaiting the command to fire. Thaddeus gripped the rail until his knuckles turned white. *This is it*, he thought. *We go down fighting.* There was no way he was going to be a prisoner again.

'READY …' bellowed Silver.

'AIM …'

'FIRE!'

But as the order tumbled from his mouth, the *Wyddah*'s starboard suddenly dipped low in the water. The cannons boomed but their deathly balls sailed over the top of the *Sea Cat* and splashed harmlessly into the water on the other side.

'WAHOOO!' shouted Thaddeus, jumping up and down on deck as Molly somersaulted out of the ocean like a dolphin.

The *Wyddah* began to drift, the current pushing her dangerously close to the pounding reef.

'HOW'D YOU LIKE THAT, PEGHEAD?' yelled Thaddeus.

'LOWER THE SHEET ANCHORS!' screamed Silver, regaining his footing.

Thaddeus leaned over the rail with a rope for Molly to climb up, but she pushed it aside.

'I think I've finally found my sea legs! Cork the ship, Thaddeus. Let's go get Juniper.'

Thaddeus shouted an order at Billy. 'Get Bones back on deck, and the three of you ready the cannons. We won't be caught out again.'

Then he jumped over the side of the *Sea Cat*. He no longer felt paralysing fear at being in the water. He had his friend and he had his ship. Both would keep him afloat. He understood now what real power was.

Molly supported him while he uncorked the bottle. The *Sea Cat* shrank and disappeared inside with a gurgle and a slurp, like bathwater down a plughole.

Silver was alternating between yelling abuse at the crew who weren't scurrying fast enough to obey his orders and screaming instructions for the *Wyddah*'s repair. The slurp of the *Sea Cat* sliding into her bottle drew his attention away from his ship and to Thaddeus and Molly, still in the open sea.

'LOWER THE BOATS!' he roared. 'GET AFTER 'EM! YE BE IN FER IT NOW, BIX!'

A few screams followed by heavy splashes informed Thaddeus and Molly that some unlucky pirates hadn't moved fast enough to do Silver's bidding.

'Hang on tight,' Molly told Thaddeus, and she skimmed them both through the water towards the reef as if she'd been doing it her whole life.

On the other side of the pounding waves, about to negotiate its way through the reef, was the longboat returning to the *Wyddah* with Captain Pepperjack and the pirates from the beach.

'Are you in for some boat-tipping?' whispered Thaddeus, his eyes alight with mischief.

Molly grinned wickedly. 'Hold on to my shoulders, and don't forget to hold your breath.'

She swam through the gap in the reef and dived deep beneath the longboat, propelled by her powerful tail. Thaddeus held up his fingers and counted off … one, two, three.

Molly rushed upwards, her arms raised, and toppled the boat sideways. The sea became alive with surprised splashes and cries. Molly's laughter exploded in bubbles around Thaddeus's face.

'Serves you right, stupid pirates,' Thaddeus taunted once he and Molly had surfaced a safe distance away.

Pepperjack looked as if he might explode

with fury. He punched Booth in the head, which gave Thaddeus a thrill. He'd hated Booth since the moment he'd told Henry to chuck Thaddeus in the sea chest.

Then he noticed the flotilla of longboats that had descended from the *Wyddah*. It wouldn't be long before they rescued their Captain and followed Thaddeus and Molly to the shore.

'Let's go,' he said to Molly.

With Thaddeus holding on tight again, Molly flicked her tail and skimmed across the shallower water of the inlet, bringing them in as close to the location of the box as her fins would allow. Thaddeus waded out and dragged her up the sand.

'Wait here and dry off so you can transform,' he told her. 'I'll get Jupe, and then we'll go across the island and relaunch the *Sea Cat* on the other side. They'll have trouble catching us if we do it that way.'

He took off across the sand towards the Unknown Grave, his heart beating erratically. He hoped he wasn't too late. The tide was coming in at an alarming rate.

He reached the patch of sand and stopped dead. The box was gone. His heart plummeted. Surely the sea hadn't already claimed it?

He dashed around in a mad circle, then

searched closer to the cliffs, hoping that maybe he'd got the location wrong. But it was no use. The box was definitely gone. And so was Juniper.

Thaddeus couldn't believe it. He fell to his knees, finding it hard to breathe. The sea had claimed Juniper instead of Pepperjack!

CHAPTER FIFTEEN

CAT AND RAT

'T HADDEUS!' screamed Molly.

He looked up. Pepperjack had swum ashore before the rest of his crew and was now holding Molly by the neck.

'Come to Pepperjack, boy,' he shouted, 'and there be no need for fish for dinner.'

Thaddeus stood and charged back along the beach. He'd lost Juniper. He couldn't lose Molly too.

Pepperjack smiled and dropped the floundering Molly onto the sand. He put a hefty boot on her belly, trapping her.

'Let her go, Pepperjack,' warned Thaddeus.

'That be Captain Pepperjack to ye, boy.'

The pirate kicked Molly towards Thaddeus, then, using his cutlass, he motioned her to stand. Thaddeus bent and helped her to her feet. Her legs had only just transformed and he could see them trembling.

'Juniper?' she whispered.

Thaddeus shook his head and heard a strangled sob escape her mouth.

Pepperjack smiled cruelly and looked out to sea. Thaddeus knew he was calculating how long it would take his crew to land. He glared at the pirate Captain's cruel face, his black pointed beard and the thick gold hoops through his ears. The pirate's fingers curled around the hilt of the cutlass were covered with skull-shaped rings of heavy silver.

Pepperjack noticed him staring. 'Be you wanting to be like Captain Pepperjack, boy? Ye've got courage and determination, which be good traits for a pirate. Maybe Pepperjack'll be giving ye a chance to join his friends aboard the *Wyddah*.'

Thaddeus snorted. 'I'm nothing like you! And you call the crew your friends? The only reason they're still here is because you bound them to you. You tricked them with your stupid contract. They didn't come here to find you, they came to get their own freedom. Stupid pirate – don't you know that friends can't be bought?' Thaddeus clenched his fists and took a step closer. 'I'll tell you about friends! Juniper was a friend to me and now he's dead because of you, you no good filthy rat!'

Molly kicked Thaddeus's leg meaningfully, but Thaddeus was on a roll of anger and guilt that had been building since he'd discovered that Juniper and the box had been swallowed by the sea. He would never see his friend again and it was all his fault. He should have held on tight to the box.

'You can keep your stinking offer,' he spat. 'Take it back to your maggoty ship and go sink yourself on some filthy reef. I'd rather die than become a rat like you!'

'You could have toned it down a bit,' whispered Molly. 'He does have a sword, remember.'

Pepperjack, his face glowing red with rage, pushed aside his jacket to reveal his other weapons.

Molly stared in dismay. 'And three more pistols!'

'Ye'll be getting your wish to die soon enough, boy,' said Pepperjack, and he prodded Thaddeus with the pointy end of his cutlass as a tide of pirates spilled from the landed longboats and surged around them.

Thaddeus realised he'd let his temper get away from him. He should have used Pepperjack's offer as a way to secure Molly's safety. He could have agreed to sign up with the stinker on one condition – that Pepperjack let Molly go. Now it was too late. Pepperjack would kill them here on the beach and leave them to become food for the crabs and gulls.

Thaddeus turned to Molly, his eyes full of regret. 'I'm sorry.'

'Oh, Captain,' gushed Silver, clomping awkwardly up the sand. 'It be workin'! The brats did be knowin' the way. Ye be free.' His face formed into a self-satisfied smirk, as if he was the one who'd orchestrated Pepperjack's release.

Thaddeus felt a new wave of anger flood through him. 'I'd watch out for Silver,' he said spitefully. 'He was hoping to be captain of the *Wyddah* himself.'

Silver turned as red as an overripe tomato about to explode beneath the hot sun.

But Pepperjack ignored the comment. 'Where be Noxious?' he asked in a steely voice.

Silver looked uncomfortable. 'He be havin' an accident, Captain. He be hangin' upside down under a spell and his wand be broken. We be havin' to tie him to a chair so his head bain't all bashed about.'

Molly snorted. 'It was no accident!'

Pepperjack's attention returned to her and

Thaddeus. 'Looks like it be fish for supper, me hearties,' he said, and the pirates cheered.

'We go down fighting,' said Thaddeus, turning so his back was against Molly's. He felt her nod, accepting their fate.

'For Juniper,' she said quietly.

'For Juniper,' echoed Thaddeus.

The pirates closed in.

Thaddeus held up his fists, ready, but the pirates didn't get any closer. They seemed suspended in mid-air for a moment before turning away.

'All-you-can-drink rum!' said one.

'Me very own Captain's hat,' said another.

'KILL THEM, YE SCURVY DOGS!' roared Pepperjack, lunging at the nearest pirate and shoving him towards Thaddeus.

Thaddeus and Molly separated and the pirate moved between them to the other side.

'GOLD!' he said in a wondering haze.

The pirates joined together in a scuffling mêlée, snapping at one another and slashing with their daggers and cutlasses.

Pepperjack dashed into the fray, yelling abuse. He pulled out his pistol and fired it. One pirate went down, but this just seemed to increase the frantic skirmish. All fifty pirates battled on, shouting nonsensical comments like 'silken robes' or 'ships galore'.

'What's going on?' asked Molly.

'I have no idea – but let's not hang around. Now's our chance.' Thaddeus turned and ran.

'Wait!' called Molly. 'There's Skip and – and he's got Juniper! JUNIPER!'

Thaddeus stopped dead. Had he heard properly? Her voice was almost drowned out by the brawling pirates. He looked to where she was pointing and couldn't believe what he saw.

Skip was on his knees, crawling between the hairy legs of the clamouring pirates. And Molly was right – Juniper was with him. Together they scrambled out of the cacophony of writhing bodies and dashed straight for Thaddeus and Molly.

Thaddeus couldn't believe it. Juniper was alive!

'How ... what ...?' He couldn't formulate the words. He just stared at his smiling friend.

'I say, I'm awfully sorry, old chap ... you know, about the box,' Juniper began.

Molly cut him off with an enormous hug.

Juniper turned pink. 'Oh, I say ... anyone would think I'd been dead.'

'You don't know the half of it,' Molly told him.

Thaddeus touched Juniper's arm. He was real alright.

Juniper gave him a worried look. 'I say, are you okay, old chap? You look like you've seen a ghost.'

'Best we get away now, while they be distracted,' interrupted Skip, gesturing towards the pirate mound, which was quickly diminishing due to Pepperjack's increasing violence.

Skip legged it down the beach and the three friends wasted no time following after him.

'What happened back there?' puffed Thaddeus, catching up with Skip. 'And where on earth did you come from?'

'I ain't be following the pirates out of the jungle,' said Skip slyly. 'Not when I be seeing Pepperjack chasing you and leaving the box behind. I always be wanting that box …'

Thaddeus stopped running. It was amazing. The whole time, it was Skip who had the box!

'So you took it and opened it?' prompted Molly.

She stopped too, and so did Skip and Juniper, all of them breathing hard.

'I be knowing it be having friendship inside, see. So yes, I be opening it – and I be right too!' Skip grinned at Juniper.

Thaddeus's mouth fell open. That was what Skip had wanted – friendship. Not treasure, or his own ship, like the other pirates.

'Well, I'm awfully glad to be out of it,' said Juniper. 'There was no food in there at all.'

'But what about the pirates?' asked Thaddeus, looking back along the beach to make sure they were all still occupied. 'Why are they fighting?'

Skip grinned. 'That be easy. Juniper be telling me that we should be sneaking up behind them and closing the box's lid. They all be wanting what's inside then, and they be fighting over it and letting us get away.'

Thaddeus stared at Juniper. He had redeemed himself in grand style.

He turned back to Skip. 'So you'll stay with us? We could sure use some help with the *Sea Cat*.'

'I can't,' said Skip sadly. 'I don't want to be a pirate no more, but I signed the Captain's contract.'

Thaddeus, Juniper and Molly didn't know what to say.

The silence was interrupted by a whining sound and a small dent appeared in the sand at their feet. Pepperjack had turned his pistols on them again.

'To the jungle!' said Thaddeus.

If they got through the cover of trees and out to the other beach, he could uncork the *Sea Cat* and then they'd be off.

'Come on, Skip – Pepperjack is shooting at you too!' said Molly, latching onto Skip's shirt and dragging him along with them.

As they zigzagged up the sand towards the opening in the dense jungle, more lead balls whizzed past their heads like angry mosquitoes.

'HIT THE SAND!' Thaddeus screamed, and dropped onto his belly. A shot whizzed past where his head had been a second ago. 'Anyone wearing a hole?' he asked, quickly checking himself before scanning his friends.

They all shook their heads.

'Follow me … and hurry!'

Thaddeus crawled army-style towards a cluster of rocks. Shots continued to whine overhead, but it wasn't much further … they were almost there … just a few more wriggles …

'That be as far as ye be going, mateys.'

Pepperjack's voice was awfully close. Thaddeus looked back in dismay. The Captain and what was left of his bruised and sullen crew were almost on top of them. They wasted no time in encircling Thaddeus's small group, pointing pistols or blades at them.

'Stand up, ye scurvy dogs. Pepperjack be the one to make ye drop,' the Captain ordered.

The bloodthirsty threat had the pirates licking their lips.

Thaddeus stood up defiantly, but Juniper staggered on wobbly legs. Skip's shoulders drooped, his eyes fixed on the sand. Molly stood tall alongside Thaddeus and glared at Pepperjack.

'Reload your weapons, me hearties,' said Pepperjack, 'and draw your daggers!'

A flurry of hands reached for powder cases, and the clink of lead shot and the scrape of blades being drawn filled the air. Thaddeus smelt gunpowder and death on the sea breeze. He looked down the beach to where a rotten portion of Pepperjack's crew lay lifeless on the sand next to the open box. Already the gulls were circling.

Thaddeus couldn't let his friends meet the same fate. As the tide crept closer, an idea formed in his brain. He placed his hand protectively over his chest, cupping the corked bottle that hung there.

'There be no room for mutineers aboard the *Black Wyddah*,' Pepperjack told Skip. 'First, Pepperjack be releasing ye from your contract. And then Pepperjack be killing ye!'

He raised his pistol and took aim at Skip's

chest.

'Is that it, Pepperjack?' Thaddeus taunted. 'Is that the biggest gun you've got?'

'THAT BE CAPTAIN PEPPERJACK TO YE!' roared Pepperjack. He placed his thumb over the pistol's hammer. 'And this be the only gun I be needing to end all your mangy lives.'

Juniper's legs gave way to jelly at the exact same moment that Thaddeus uncorked the bottle. His ears rang with the roar of Pepperjack's pistol firing … but the pirate was too late. The *Sea Cat* swept out of her bottle faster than lightning and swept them up onto the safety of her deck.

'I say, that was close.' Juniper wiped his shiny face with his sleeve.

'I be needing to get back to the Captain,' Skip said sadly. He was visibly trembling.

'Oh no, you don't,' said Thaddeus. 'You heard Pepperjack. He said he released you from your contract!'

Skip looked stunned, then quickly pulled back his ear to reveal the spot where the black tattoo had sat. 'Be the *Wyddah* gone?' he asked urgently.

'I say, Skip, there's nothing there,' said Juniper. 'The mark's gone!'

It took a moment for Skip to register Juniper's words, then he whooped for joy. The others joined in.

'That was pretty clever, Thaddeus,' said Molly appreciatively.

Billy appeared, wearing a worried expression. 'There be no time for celebratin' when ye be goin' and beachin' us, Cap'n.'

'Only for a while, Billy. Look at the tide – it's coming in fast.'

Thaddeus peered over the rail, straight into the furious gaze of Pepperjack. He could also see some squashed legs of a few unfortunate pirates who hadn't made it out of the way of the *Sea Cat*.

'Still thinking that's the only gun you need, you stinking pirate?' he yelled to the Captain, then turned back to his own crew. 'Ready the cannons.'

His friends whooped and raced to the *Sea Cat*'s gun ports.

Thaddeus looked down at Pepperjack again and felt a triumphant flush when he saw real fear in the pirate's eyes. The *Sea Cat*'s cannon ports opened with a bang and two angry black noses jutted out.

'This is what I call a gun, you maggoty rat!' Thaddeus shouted.

'RUN FOR YOUR LIVES!' yelled Silver.

'Take aim,' shouted Thaddeus. 'FIRE!'

The cannons boomed and Thaddeus almost

wet his pants laughing at the sight of Pepperjack and his crew speeding off down the beach chased by cannon balls.

The pirates reached the patch of sand where the Unknown Grave was located and stopped. They were out of range of the *Sea Cat*'s cannons, but couldn't go any further because of the sheer cliffs. Pepperjack's fury washed over his crew like a tidal wave.

Thaddeus leant against the *Sea Cat*'s rail and enjoyed the show. Bones picked up his violin and began playing a jaunty tune. The Sad Lady wafted by and Thaddeus could have sworn he saw the merest hint of a smile on her lips.

Pip wafted over with a bucket of popcorn and sat next to Thaddeus. 'Look at 'ims, Cap'n. He be real mad now. He almost be choppin' 'ems heads off.' And he stuffed a handful of popcorn in his mouth and chomped happily.

'They'll be back, you know,' said Molly, joining them. 'They'll wait till after dark and then they'll spread out and creep back.'

'She be right, Captain,' warned Skip.

'It doesn't matter,' said Thaddeus, feeling a small glow at Skip's use of the title. 'Look at the tide. Pretty soon the *Sea Cat*'s hull will be underwater. In the meantime, Juniper, you're in charge of the cannons. Get Bones and the Sad Lady to help you – and shoot anything that comes within range.'

'What's about me, Cap'n, what's about me?' Pip was now dancing dangerously along the ship's rail.

'You go up to the nest and yell out if any one of those manky pirates takes even a single step towards us.'

'Aye, aye, Cap'n,' shouted Pip, wafting upwards, his buttery face turned towards the cliffs.

'Molly, Skip, ready the sails,' Thaddeus said. 'As soon as the hull is covered with water, lower them. The wind should do the rest.'

'But the reef – we'll never make it through,' said Molly.

'I think we will. Look how high the tide is – it'll make it easier to get through the gap. Besides, we have no other choice.'

He turned to Billy. 'You go to the stern and keep an eye on the tide. Ahoy when she's ready to go.'

Billy's misty form wafted to the stern, passing straight through the mainmast in his hurry.

'They won't catch us now,' Thaddeus said. 'They'll be stranded here for days while they fix the *Wyddah*'s hull.'

'If I be knowing Silver, he'll be having the Sea Witch fix it already,' Skip warned. 'She be bound to the *Wyddah* still, which means she must be doing the bidding of the Captain or face death.'

The children looked across the water towards the *Black Wyddah*. Skip was right – the ship no longer looked like it was listing to one side.

'We failed the Sea Witch,' said Thaddeus. He'd been so caught up in the fight with Pepperjack that he'd forgotten all about his bargain with her.

'How's your arm?' asked Molly.

'Achy, but not too bad.'

'Then you ain't failed her. You just be delaying your promise,' said Skip.

'But we didn't bury the box. And now Pepperjack's escaped … but she's still chained to the *Wyddah*. Burying the box was the only way we knew how to set her free,' Thaddeus finished in a low voice. He didn't want to upset Juniper.

'There be other ways to free her. We just have to find them,' Skip said.

Thaddeus looked at him questioningly, but any further conversation was cut short by Billy's yell.

'Hull be buried, Cap'n!'

'This is it – drop the mainsail,' Thaddeus called to Molly and Skip. He had his fingers crossed. Would the plan work?

The *Sea Cat* became a hive of activity. The sails fell with heavy snaps, and fluttered momentarily before swallowing the wind and billowing outwards with full, heavy bellies. The *Sea Cat* groaned as she inched her way into deeper water.

Pepperjack realised what was going on. 'AFTER THEM, YE IMBECILES, OR I'LL BE MAROONING THE LOT OF YE!'

The pirates darted towards the floating ship, but Juniper, the Sad Lady and the fiddler let loose a volley of cannon balls. They spurted sand up around the pirates as they landed. The pirates hesitated, and some ran back to the safety of the cliffs – where Pepperjack began shooting at them.

'WHAT BE YE STARING AT?' he roared, pointing his pistols at his remaining crew. 'EITHER YE BE DODGING CANNON BALLS OR YE BE FEELING ME PISTOLS IN YER BELLIES.'

It was easier to dodge the cannon fire. The pirates surged towards the *Sea Cat* again.

'They're coming,' warned Molly.

'Let them,' said Thaddeus.

Nothing could ruin this moment. The *Sea Cat*'s sails were full and she was skimming across the waves towards the gap in the reef. Everyone on board sucked in their breath, as if this might give her extra room. They needn't have worried. The *Sea Cat* slipped through with room to spare and sailed out into deeper water.

Thaddeus whooped with joy. He ran to the stern and poked his tongue out at the furious Pepperjack and his crew.

The pirates had finally reached the longboats and were rowing towards the *Wyddah* as fast as they could in the *Sea Cat*'s wake. Pepperjack stood at the bow of one longboat and fired his pistol at Thaddeus. The shot missed by a mile.

'Is that all you've got, you stinking loser?' Thaddeus taunted.

He put his hands either side of his face and waved his fingers, then blew a big fat raspberry at Pepperjack. He considered mooning the angry Captain, but restrained himself and settled on more verbal abuse instead.

'You can't catch me, you big fat stinking pirate. Your big fat old boat is slower than a wet weekend!'

Pepperjack jumped up and down with rage. Unable to take his wrath out on Thaddeus, he picked up two of his men and tossed them from the longboat into the *Sea Cat*'s churning wake.

He might have lost his whole crew this way had the wind not suddenly changed, bringing with it a droop in the *Sea Cat*'s sails.

A smile as bright as the sun chased away the thunderclouds on Pepperjack's face. 'ROW, YE SCURVY DOGS, WE'LL CATCH 'EM YET!' he roared, and pointed his pistol at his sweating crew, threatening to shoot anyone who slowed.

The pirates reached the *Wyddah* and, leaving the longboats to drift, Pepperjack and his crew shinnied up the ropes and leapt onto their ship's deck.

Thaddeus still wasn't bothered. The wind was returning and the *Sea Cat* had a good head-start and she was a lighter and faster vessel. Besides, Pepper's diminished crew hadn't even unfurled the *Wyddah*'s sails yet.

Juniper appeared by Thaddeus's side. 'I say, what now, old chap?'

'Now you get out your Buccaneers Chart and think about a place called Anatolia.'

'We're going to get his mother's dreams,' said Molly.

Thaddeus nodded and grinned. Then he leapt up onto the rail and held one of the *Sea Cat*'s three massive stern lanterns for balance. He waved his hand to catch Pepperjack's attention.

'Who's afraid of the teeny black rat? Not the *Sea Cat*!' he chanted.

He knew Pepperjack had heard him because the pirate captain shot Booth in the foot. Thaddeus whooped and continued his song, hoping for more casualties. Pretty soon Pepperjack might be the only able seaman aboard the *Wyddah*.

Juniper's brow creased with worry. 'I say, old chap, I know you're the Captain and all that, but do you really have to torment him? He'll never give up now – he'll come after us if it's the last thing he ever does. It'll be the end of us.'

The wind returned with a gust that tousled Thaddeus's red hair along with the sails, giving him a roguish look.

'Have you ever seen a rat eat a cat?' he asked.

Juniper shook his head.

'Nor have I,' said Thaddeus with a grin. 'That's why it can't be the end, Jupe. I think it's only just the beginning.'

~ THE END ~

(not)

Acknowledgements

A lot of time and energy, emotional investment and practical effort goes into helping a book sail off into the wide world.

I'd like to thank a number of people for helping me breathe life into the sails of *Thaddeus Bix and the Pirates of Pepperjack*.

To my Mum and Dad, my brothers Daniel, Simon and Matthew, and my sisters-in-law Leah and Marlyn, for encouraging me to be true to myself and reminding me that my passions in life are worthwhile ventures.

To the four people I love the most in this world: Alena, Phoebe, Charlotte and Lachlan Mansfield, who inspired me to write for children in the first place.

To my Grandparents and to Aaron and Jasmine Gibbs, for their unfailing support in everything, and who refused to let me doubt and repeated the mantra 'Just do it!'

A big thank you to Deborah-Dawn Risley and Margaret Fortmann for reading some early and confusing drafts and offering helpful opinions on how to refine the story. Also thank you to Deborah-Dawn Risley, Ella Risley, Anne Johns and Jebediah Johns for assisting me in the final proofreading along with Gwennyth Manser and Pauline O'Carolan.

A huge thank you to Rachel Farren for all of her

help at the book fair, and to Amber Heeney for dealing with a meltdown and ensuring that this story made it to the bookshelves. Also a big thanks to Julia Jurevicius for her late-night efforts with my grammatical quandaries and her continuous encouragement.

Behind the scenes of every printed work there are these invisible people called editors. They polish words and sentences and make them all shiny. I have been privileged to work with three of these wonderful and very patient people. First of all, thank you to Selena Hanet-Hutchins of Texture, who has inspired and encouraged me with my writing for years. Her editorial advice has been invaluable. To Elizabeth Hyndman of Pro-editing: your honesty gave me courage. And to Nicola O'Shea of ebookedit, thank you for the huge final edits and for helping Thaddeus Bix come to life. Without your time this story would still be buried within a file on my laptop!

I would also like to express my immense gratitude to the very talented Jurevicius brothers, Nathan and Luke, for their joint effort on the cover art: Nathan for the beautiful artwork, and Luke for the layout, text and highlighting. People say you should never judge a book by its cover, but in this case I think you most certainly should!

A big thanks also to Keith Stevenson of ebookedit for the formatting of both the ebook and print book.

Finally, a huge thank you to my readers. You give a story its one true purpose – to be heard.

About the author

Kylie Mansfield lives in South Australia, where she writes women's contemporary and children's fantasy fiction. Both genres reflect her real-life love of and fascination with ancient stories, old rambling houses, whispered secrets, mythology, and enable her to traverse many fantastical worlds through the doorway of her imagination.

Kylie comes from a family of avid storytellers and book lovers, and for as long as she can remember she has amused, soothed and entranced herself with stories. *Thaddeus Bix and the Pirates of Pepperjack* is her first published work.

You can find more information about Kylie and her books at http://kyliemansfield.com.

Facebook:
https://www.facebook.com/writerkyliemansfield/

Twitter:
https://twitter.com/kyliemans

Instagram:
https://www.instagram.com/kyliemans/

Goodreads:
https://www.goodreads.com/
goodreadscomKylieMansfield

Amazon author page:
http://www.amazon.com/Kylie-Mansfield/e/
B01DMRWRWQ?ref_=pe_1724030_132998060

CPSIA information can be obtained
at www.ICGtesting.com
Printed in the USA
LVHW011930180520
655843LV00003B/216